Gritty, Grisly and Greedy

Crimes and Characters Inspired by 20 Years as a Fed

Stuart Scott

Moscow, Idaho

i

Gritty, Grisly and Greedy

Crimes and Characters Inspired by 20 Years as a Fed

Stuart Scott
Moscow, Idaho

Published by
Stuart Scott
112 S. Main St.
Moscow, Idaho

Copyright Stuart Scott, 2018

CreateSpace Edition
ISBN# 978-1-7322468-1-2

Cover Design by: Clarissa Yeo/ Yocla Designs

Preface

You are about to read stories inspired by real people, true crimes and actual events from my 28-year career. Overlapping my years as a fed were 20 years, between active and reserve duty, as an Army CID agent. The true events in my stories are woven into narratives involving other actual events. The bank robbery incidents are all true. The quirky people, the nation's first gay riot and two mass-shooting scenarios are true events where I chose to involve my characters. The state hospitals or prisons depicted are places I visited.

Among the more recognizable cases that my career touched are: Patty Hearst, Richard Butler of the Aryan Nations movement, Timothy Boyce the spy, Randy Weaver of Ruby Ridge and Sarah Jane Moore. In choosing what to write I followed two rules. The stories were to have some moments of humor, with black humor, plot twists and sympathetic characters where possible. Second, my stories should be unique and never just cheap imitations of other tales already told.

Stuart Scott

Contents

To my wife, Susan

1. The Tooth Fairy

Spokane, Washington, is a cold place in winter. But I learned to deal with it because, like the shark I am, I've got to keep moving...or die.

My clients will have found shelter somewhere by now. I frequently find them under the Interstate 90 overpass, just south of First Street. Outside the Union Gospel Mission is always a good bet. By the women's shelter is also good. We always manage to find enough privacy to conduct our quick business transactions.

If I spot a cardboard sign, "Homeless—Please help—God Bless." I'm in. We'll move away from their street corner—for privacy—and get down to business.

You learn to spot the ones that are working. The outfits change from the standard hooker mini-skirt summer uniform to a short winter parka over skirts and leggings. Their 'tell' is the 'hard stare.' Somewhere there must be a book, Street Whore 101 or Hooking for Dummies, something like that. Anyway, they all have the hard stare down pat. If you look back as you pass, they know you're looking, and you know they're working. I stay away from the better-dressed ladies. They aren't interested in what I've got in mind.

My clients don't have the hard stare down very well at all. They're reminded of the beatings they've taken: from their boyfriend or their dad, take your pick. Anyway, they look at me for a few seconds at most and then look away. But they always look back. Hunger, cold or a craving are all powerful aphrodisiacs. That's when I know I've got 'em!

I've got to admit I like male clients best. Nothing against the ladies, mind you, but guys are just much more straightforward. I tell them what I'm interested in and what I can pay. Then I get a straight answer, no drama. Yes or no. These guys understand what it takes to get by and I can respect that.

By now I can pretty much tell who to ask and who to pass. We find some privacy and then it's down on their knees, mouths open and I'm in. I always make sure I've washed my tool before I put it in their mouth. Courteous, right? It never takes me too long, probably two minutes and I'm finished. I wipe off and put it away, pay and leave. I'm polite and don't stiff anybody on the price. That would just be wrong. After all, I'm getting what I want, plus I don't need a bad rap on the street.

My name is Vince. I buy gold teeth, and that's how I got my nick name—The Tooth Fairy.

* * *

Harry sat across the table from Wendell, his new boss. Harry had been hired to help Wendell at the crematorium. Taking the new man out for a meal was probably meant to motivate him to be a reliable employee. Tonight was Harry's introduction to the job: dinner and a demonstration.

"I'm looking forward to tonight's dinner. I absolutely love fresh seafood. Opening my own mussels and oysters, peeling the shrimp, cracking open a crab, it doesn't get any better than that." Wendell looked at Harry, expecting...*what? Enthusiasm? I bet he'll start smacking his lips any minute now,* Harry thought, smiling as he looked across the table.

"Let me show you how to open one of these up." Wendell leaned over the table, knife in hand. "A little cut here on this side and on the opposite side. That's all there is to it. Now put your fingers into the opening, one hand on the top and one on the bottom."

Harry's eyes shifted from his boss's face to the grasping hands.

"Now, one sharp yank and it's open." Pointing with his finger, Wendell smiled at his companion, "and here we are— four real beauties."

2

Harry's kept his expression blank as Wendell, pliers in hand, began pulling out the four gold crowns that adorned the back corners of the corpse's upper and lower jaws. Each molar made a soft plunking sound as Wendell dropped it into a small plastic tub that had once held sour cream.

"Now, help me slide him into the oven, then we're out of here and off to dinner."

Wendell lifted the body by its upper arms while Harry grabbed the legs. The crematory oven had a heavy steel tray that rolled out. Harry could see the blue and yellow glow of the pilot light at the far end of the u-shaped gas jets that enfolded the rolling tray. The rollers bumped the stops as the tray slid to the end of the tracks. Wendell lifted the counter-weighted handle, and the brick-lined door of the furnace descended. Turning the handle on the gas valve, Harry could hear a muted hiss. When Wendell pushed the red igniter button on the wall, the pop of the gas and the roar of flames around the body caused Harry to pull back from the small window in the door of the oven.

"Just like baking a cake, partner, only hotter and longer. Now come on, let's go get that dinner!"

* * *

Like with any other business in a market economy, commodity prices—be it gold or pork bellies—vary. I check the house newspapers kicking around Mindy's, my favorite diner. All the papers have the latest price on gold. Fortunately for me, I've always had a head for business, and enough self-discipline to stay out of debt and avoid expensive filthy habits. Cheap filthy habits on the other hand, are an entirely different thing.

I keep my overhead low and have a regular customer who buys my gold. This is my third year in business, and I keep growing. I pay $50 per tooth, either in cash or pharmaceutical treats. I also pay $5 for a referral, so it's a win-win for my

3

regulars when they bring me a new client. I'm always in the market for new clients and have expanded my area to include the reservation towns that circle Spokane. After all, how many gold crowns can one wino have?

Over the years, I've refined and simplified both my equipment and my approach. Equipment was a problem for my first year but finally a simple solution came to mind. Six-inch vice-grip pliers work perfectly well for street corner dentistry. Who'd have guessed! My last addition was a van, an oldie but a goodie for 'mobile work'.

Anyway, my full name is Vince Farmer. My two associates are Wendell Gruber and Harry Brill. I first met Wendell and Harry at Robert Smiley's coin shop in Coeur d'Alene, Idaho, where I sell my gold. Wendell and Harry are also in the gold business. Well, actually they're in the cremation business, but they extract gold teeth from the stiffs who pass through the crematorium.

When I walked into the coin shop and met them for the first time, Wendell was two-thirds of the way through telling a joke. He loved to tell 'Jew jokes.'

"The first old Jew says, 'My business of thirty-five years was destroyed in a fire, so I decided to retire.'

"And the second Jew says, 'I understand; forty years Sarah and I had the clothing store and we got wiped out by a flood.'

"A long pause, then the first Jew asks, 'So, how do you start a flood?'"

I waited for Wendell to stop laughing at his own humor and then introduced myself. Robert and Harry weren't laughing at all.

Wendell leaned into Robert and whispered in his ear. I couldn't hear his question, but it became clear soon enough as Robert answered for all to hear.

"No, I'm sure Vince is okay. You can talk in front of him. He buys gold teeth from the winos in Spokane. He's part of the same food chain as you two, except he's fishing a little up-stream, so to speak." That seemed to relax the two.

"They also recycle precious metal," clarified Robert, without going into any detail.

I glanced from Wendell to Robert and back. "So the gold you're selling, it's recycled?"

"Exactly," responded Wendell.

"So how did you get into this niche of recycling?" Wendell asked, seeming to want to validate Robert's endorsement of me.

"My dad was a bookie in San Francisco. He taught me that a man had to be as good as his word. Anyway, he committed to paying a debt and once, when he came up short, he pulled out his own gold tooth to cover what he owed."

Wendell seemed impressed enough that it silenced him for a moment before he finally responded.

"Wow, that's a great story. What a stand-up guy your dad was. I'm impressed."

"How about you?" I smiled and focused my gaze, signaling that he had my full attention.

"Hey, I got nothing that even comes close. I'm working in the mortuary crematorium, watching bodies get turned into ashes. So anyway, it just comes to me one day. Why not? I mean, we're going to vaporize the stuff anyway, and there you go."

"Well, let's see what you've got. Vince, why don't you go first?" Robert said.

I pulled the plastic bag from my jacket pocket and emptied the contents onto Robert's counter. Out tumbled a cluster of crumpled gold crowns that had once been on thirty-one different teeth. They had been smashed with a hammer to crush the teeth they had covered. Freeing them from the teeth had made them look like so many bright gold raisins. Hammered and then soaked in peroxide, they had lost all

5

traces of their former shapes and their former owners. I watched silently as Robert counted and weighed my collection.

I'd checked before I came in and today's spot price for gold was $1,209 per ounce. I had a good buyer, but I'd be foolish not to do my own due diligence before selling on a commodities exchange. I liked doing business here. I get 85 percent of the spot gold price, and he pays based on an average purity of 80 percent, or 20 karats. It's a fair price.

Robert smiled across the counter as he pulled over his calculator. The blue numbers on the scale blinked. The digital reader board above his head displayed a continual update of precious metal prices, Gold $1209—Silver $16.80.

"78 grams. Nice haul, my friend. That weight puts you at 2.7337 ounces and at 85 percent purity brings us back to 2.3237 ounces. Now for the adjustment to 20 karat, so 80 percent purity takes us to 1.8587 ounces of pure gold. That's what you've got. I'll cut you a check for $2247.23 if you're ready to sell."

I nodded in agreement. I already knew what I should be getting before I came in, and Robert knew that I knew, so it was an expedient process.

"It's always a pleasure to do business with you, Robert." I took the check and left. After expenses, I'd just cleared $697.23 for three days work. It could have been more, depending on the price of gold, but hey, we all have bills to pay.

* * *

"Ow—ow," Alice moaned as I withdrew my pliers and her gold-crowned molar. We were in the back of my van. Alice was kneeling on a carpet square at my feet.

"Here, wet your finger. Dip it in this and rub it on the socket. It will kill the pain and help stop the bleeding." I held open a ginger Altoid tin that I used for my cocaine stash.

6

"Now bite down on this." I passed her half of a junior size tampon. "And keep your jaw closed on that for the next twenty minutes so your blood will clot. You can get up now."

With her jaw clamped firmly shut, Alice sat on the folding chair I kept in the van. I'd keep her here for the twenty minutes and give her some instruction while we waited. Alice slumped forward in the chair, her head resting in the palm of her hand as I talked.

"Four things are all you have to remember. Stick to soup or soft foods for one solid week. Don't brush, but clean your mouth by swishing with wine or booze. If you start to bleed, repeat what you're doing now. Don't take any aspirin for two weeks. Okay, do you understand what I just said?"

I got no response from Alice, so I put my hand on her shoulder, intending to shake her if the touch of my hand alone was not enough. Then her head slipped off her hand and she slumped over, her head almost touching her knees. I'm thinking, *Jesus, the broad's passed out.* When she fell out of the chair, I knew she had passed out. Unfortunately for us both, I was wrong. She was dead.

"Shit—shit—shit!"

＊＊＊

I parked in the alley and walked to the crematorium. I could hear Wendell through the door.

"Harry, have you heard the one about what Hitler said to Mussolini when he visited Berlin?" Wendell was already laughing at his own joke. Harry didn't respond.

"Hitler says, 'If I'd of known you were coming, I'd have baked a Kike," and Wendell roars with laughter. Harry didn't say anything and only shook his head. Wendell's laughter is cut short by my pounding on the back door.

"Hey. It's Vince, right? This is unexpected, come in. Harry, look, it's Vince from the pawn shop." Harry's got nothing to say, which seems to be fine with Wendell. He clearly prefers the sound of his own voice anyway.

"So, what's up? We've not had you at our place before. Welcome." Wendell notices my glances around the room, and back outside to the alley and the van.

"Listen guys, I need to ask a favor. I've got something that needs to go in your oven. Can you help me out?" Looks are exchanged, Wendell to Harry—Harry to his newspaper—Wendell to me.

"What do you think?" Wendell says, turning to Harry. Harry looks up from the comics and shrugs.

"Okay, what have you got there, Vince?"

"Can you give me a hand?" I asked. "It's a big load."

"No problem. Harry, open the oven and get the tray out while I help Vince with the load."

We opened the two rear doors of the van and there lay Alice. In life she had been a big woman, and death had only managed to amplify her weight if not her size.

"What the hell happened?"

"Heart attack, probably, I'd just done her extraction. She'd dabbed coke onto the socket and I had her just sit there while her blood clotted."

"Why burn her? Why not just drive up to Mount Spokane and dump her? Take her to the Sacred Heart Emergency room and dump her out. Pulling teeth isn't illegal after all."

"I gave her coke to put on her jaw, and I traded coke for the crown. I don't want to chance the attention that an emergency room drop or a found body might bring. I didn't see anyone around when she got in the van, and I found her myself today so she wasn't a referral. I just need her to disappear."

"Okay then," said Wendell, as he reached into the van.

I went in through the side door and grabbed her feet while Wendell went to grab Alice under her arms. Harry held the door to the shop open.

"Jeez, what a beast," commented Wendell, "and she weighs a ton. What a porker."

Alice just looked up, her dead eyes sunk deep in her fat. She probably wouldn't have liked Wendell any better than he seemed to like her.

Wendell tried to heft Alice, then shook his head. "I say we two-part her. It'll make her a lot easier to move. I've got an electric chain saw here in the shop that we can use, quick and quiet."

"Look, we'll drag her inside if we have to, but we're not cutting up a body outside in an alley. I don't care how heavy she is. Once we're inside, Harry can help us get her up onto the tray. Just hurry up."

Wendell continued to grumble but managed to pull Alice out of the van and ease her to the ground. Sacrificing decorum for speed, we hauled Alice into the crematorium by her feet and Harry closed the door.

"Will you look at that," Wendell snickered at the many rolls and folds of Alice's skin. She had not been wearing panties under her heavy wool skirt.

With Wendell at her head, Harry under the rump and me lifting her legs, we got Alice onto the steel tray that was sticking out from the interior of the large gas oven.

"Vince, she's a big woman, and she'll take a shit load of gas to reduce her down. I've got to get some help with the cost; just for the gas now, you understand."

"How much?" I had no ability to negotiate.

"The going rate is a dollar a pound. I'm guessing that we've got 250 pounds, on the hoof, easy. You good with that? It's only fair," Wendell said, with his hands out, palms up, as he tried to look pitiful.

"How did you come up with the dollar a pound?"

"That was what my former boss at the vet clinic charged for his cremations. So I figured—"

9

"Whatever," I interrupted, realizing I didn't really want to know, "Just burn her."

"Okay, done. Harry, roll her on in and close the door."

When the gas jets whooshed, the signal that Alice was soon to be gone, I forked over the money for the gas and started through the door.

"Wait—wait! Vince, did the old bag have any more gold teeth?"

I had nothing to say and neither did Harry as I got into my van and drove away.

* * *

It was mid-January, and the sky was gray with snow in the air, just about to fall. I'd parked the van next to my favorite bar, The Jones Radiator Company. My route took me east on Sprague, all the way to Zips fast food joint, while I looked for business. Then I turned down the alley that parallels Sprague and worked my way back to the van.

The alleys are as good as the hooker stroll on Sprague for finding teeth. The homeless, the winos and especially the hopeless have their own routes for travel. To and from their flops or hidey-holes: to the soup kitchen, the stroll or the begging corners. They pass us, travelling parallel, yet apart from the rest of the citizenry.

The figure came out of the shadow of a dumpster just ahead on my right. At first I thought he might represent new business. Head down and topped with a dirty wool cap, his hands in the pockets of his parka. We could have been brothers, dressed alike by our mother, except my wool cap was clean and my parka wasn't patched with duct tape. My hands were also thrust deep into my pockets. I clutched vice grips in one hand and the Altoid tin of coke in the other. His hands were also deep in his pockets, but as I was soon to discover, one clutched a knife.

"Hey man, can you spare a couple of bucks so I can get something to eat at Zips?" His mouth showed the rotten and missing teeth of a chronic meth user.

Unlike downtown shoppers or tourists, I wasn't someone who crossed the street when I noticed a guy like this. Business was business, if not now, maybe tomorrow. Or, if not with him, maybe with someone he'd send to me. So, reluctantly I took my hand out from the deep warmth of my parka pocket and went for my wallet. I took out five bucks and passed it over.

"Here, go get something to eat and there's a buck for coffee. They call me the Tooth Fairy. I've got a way you could make some better money, if you're interested."

"You queer, man? Want me to cop your joint?"

His thinking I might be vulnerable or at least not a straight citizen seemed to embolden him. He stepped closer and the knife emerged in the other hand. My own hand tightened on the vice grips still out of sight in my pocket.

"Give me the wallet, Tinker Bell," he said, as the knife came up in front of my face.

He was looking for fear in my eyes when he should have been watching my hands. Out came my other hand, the pliers hidden by my palm. I stepped into him and with a side-arm slap, hit him as hard as I could on the temple. It caught him just below his wool cap and the metal of the vice grips tore his skin. I watched him fall to his knees. Dropping the knife, he put his hand to his face as I opened the pliers and clamped them shut on his nose.

I couldn't tell what he was screaming, just that it was loud and I didn't want any attention. Bending over, I pushed the vice grips to the slushy asphalt of the alley. His body followed until he lay at my feet, his face and body in the cold slush. I pulled down on the vice grips, forcing his nose to his upper lip, and the yelling stopped. It looked like his eyes, or at least the one I could see, were watering. The knife lay in the slush a few feet from his body.

11

"You ungrateful little shit-weasel, I should kill you for that," I said, and I twisted his nose. Blood was now leaking from around the jaws of the pliers as he tried to scream but only succeeded in blowing bubbles into the slush.

"Here's what happens now." My heart rate returned toward normal. "I'm going to let you live. If anyone asks what happened to you, you'll say, 'I slipped on the ice and fell.' My gun is in my other pocket, but you are such a low-life pussy I knew I wouldn't need it this time."

He didn't know that I was lying about a gun and with him on the ground, it probably didn't matter.

"Next time I see you, you're going to run in the opposite direction. And if anyone tries to jack me again, I'm going to think you set it up. Then I'll find you and show you real pain. I'll put the pliers on all your soft parts including every finger and toe. Tell me you understand?"

"Yes...yes I understand," he said, as best he could, with his face and part of his mouth still in the slush.

I popped the release inside the handle of the vice grips and put them back in my pocket. I bent over and picked up his knife, a cheap Buck knock-off. The smell of urine rose to my nose and I could see a small trail of steam rising from his crotch, where warm urine met the cold slush. He'd pissed himself.

"I'm going west down the alley and you're going east as fast as you can, now beat it."

He did.

* * *

The door to the crematorium was unlocked so I knocked and let myself in. Wendell was trying to tell a joke, but kept breaking the rhythm by interrupting with his own laughter.

"So, the Camp Commandant says, 'Lippschitz, the good news is you are being given a position in the General's household. You will no longer be cold or hungry and you'll be surrounded by beautiful women.

"'So what's the bad news?' asked Lippschitz.

"'You're going as a lamp shade,'" Wendell roared with laughter again. Harry just shook his head and said nothing.

"Mr. Vince, hey, welcome. Thanks for coming in so we could talk."

"No problem Wendell, what's up?" I asked, as I shed my parka and cap.

"Vince, I've got some good news and some bad news." Wendell seemed to speak with alternating seriousness and smirks. "I got the cost wrong on the body disposal I did for you. It should have been more for the fat broad, so I'm going to need another $250. That's the bad news. But the good news for you is I'm going to keep your secret, and it's only going to cost you the same $250 every month."

"This is a joke, right? Wendell, you trying to put the arm on me?" I asked, as I stepped closer.

"Hey, it's a fair price. You don't need the aggravation the cops would bring to your business, with the coke and all." Wendell now had his hands raised, palms out, as I had invaded his personal space. Harry seemed content just to watch.

"You really want to do this?"

"Vince, come on now, think of it as the cost of doing business. I'll tell you what, for the same price, I'll burn the next stiff you bring in, free, call it a... professional courtesy. How's that now?" Wendell smiled broadly, like he'd just given me a huge gift.

"I'll tell you how that is." I punched him: three short, hard blows to the body. Wendell fell back, knocked off his feet. His head hit the corner of the metal tray that stuck out from the open crematory oven. He didn't get up as blood pooled on the floor from the back of his head.

13

I looked at Harry. He shrugged and uncharacteristically, he spoke.

"Next to home, statistically most accidents occur in the work place. Did I ever tell you that my dad's name was Brillstein when he emigrated after the war? True story. If he told about one more Jew joke, I might have killed him myself. Thanks, you saved me the trouble," and with that, Harry offered me his hand to shake.

"That's a funny thing. My dad's name was Farmacus. He was Greek but he shortened it to Farmer when he got here. Back then being Greek was nothing you wanted to advertise. Anyways, can we put him on the tray?"

"Absolutely," said Harry, as we worked together to heft Wendell onto the tray and roll him into the oven. I shut the oven door and Harry turned on the gas while I looked through the small viewing port in the oven door.

"Harry, I think he's moving."

"Too late," intoned Harry, as he hit the igniter button. The whoosh of the flames as the gas ignited blotted out any other sound from within the oven.

I turned away from the oven door and looked at Harry. He was whistling. I recognized the tune, "If I'da Known You Were Coming I'd of Baked a Cake."

"Do you think anyone will miss Wendell?"

"Hum," Harry mumbled as he thought for a minute. "Maybe Christine, the whore who works the corner of First and Napa? I can't think of anyone else. If it comes up I'll show them his note." He walked over to the small desk in the corner of the office and wrote on a piece of binder paper.

He held up the note for me to see. "I'm tired of dead bodies. I quit!!!" and it was signed, "Wendell Shicklgruber."

"I thought his name was Gruber?"

"Yeah" replied Harry. "After a couple of Jew jokes one day, dear Wendell explained that his parents had dropped the 'Shickle' when they came to the states in '47. I remember the

14

way he said it and his grin, because it seemed more like a boast."

"What do you say we merge our businesses, Harry? I'll help with pickup and the firing if you need me. When the shop's not busy, I'll work my route. What do you think?

"Sounds like a plan to me, Vince. Sounds like a plan."

The End

Author's Notes

The Tooth Fairy is based on two parolees. One operated a coin shop and did trade drugs for gold. The other, the basis for the Wendell character, was a member of the Aryan Nations white supremacist group and liked to tell "Jew jokes."

2. The Easter Massacre Mystery

Prologue

George McIntyre found a quiet spot on a brush-covered Pullman hillside on that Easter Sunday in 1949. He had already left Officer Ross Claar dead on the ground at a Main Street filling station, and more were about to fall. It was kill or be killed on that Easter afternoon.

The gas station attendant saw Claar gunned down and called the city police. Deputies Davis and Gallagher, from the five-man Whitman County Sheriff's Department, were radioed a warning about the shooting by county dispatch. Arriving in Pullman, they parked below McIntyre's house to block any possible escape. McIntyre had already left his house for the hiding place across the street. He had brought with him an 8mm German sniper rifle with a powerful scope, range finder binoculars, and plenty of ammunition. As Gallagher stepped out of his car, a single shot from McIntyre's rifle ended his life. Davis was the next target, a bullet wound in the arm putting him out of action.

McIntyre swiftly moved up a nearby hill that was covered in a thick growth of head-high brush. His experience as an army sniper in Europe told him that concealment for a shooter was good. Any attempt to approach him would neither be fast nor quiet.

McIntyre saw two men standing at the top of the hill talking and overheard them discussing his possible position. Moments later, the man in the dark blue brimmed cap, Ernest Buck, was shot twice and killed. Ernest was a local taxi driver. His official-looking cap had cost him his life. The second civilian, Jim Roberts, managed to hide behind a car. McIntyre shot Roberts twice but Roberts survived.

A call for help from the Whitman County prosecutor brought all hands from local law enforcement to the scene. Moscow, Idaho, eight miles away, sent two officers. The Washington State Patrol had one trooper minutes away and more coming from over an hour away in Spokane. The surviving members of the Pullman city and Whitman County departments, a total of seven men, were there. When Whitman County Sheriff Pete Parnell arrived on the scene, a bullet to the heart killed him as he stepped from his car. Together the assembled law officers numbered nine men—probably not enough for the job.

Soon, the call went out to the public for trained men willing to step into harm's way. Officers called personal friends they knew as skilled hunters, target shooters or veterans studying under the G.I. bill at Washington State College. With four dead and two more wounded, every man with guts and a gun was asked to assemble in the shelter of two metal grain silos on the Palouse Highway

The nine officers, bolstered by a posse of roughly 30 volunteers, eased out from behind the shelter of the silos. Slowly they moved out in small groups. Some set out to flank the sniper's hillside nest to the north and south. One group drove away from the scene, up above and behind McIntyre into the College Hill section of Pullman, on the east side of the sniper. A few chose to aim their guns from behind the cover of the cars and an earth berm that lined the Palouse Highway to McIntyre's west.

Thirty minutes later the shooting began. No one knows who gave the signal to start, but in the next forty minutes, more than a hundred shots were fired before the posse's guns fell silent. Two more shots rang out, then silence again. At six o'clock, the news that George McIntyre was dead spread throughout the groups. Posse members carried him down the hill to the gravel yard outside the silos. Hunters and gawkers— men, women and even children—encircled the body. Some stepped forward to nudge the body with their shoes, like the corpse of a dead animal, fearsome when alive, but theirs to stand over in death.

"Who shot him?" bystanders asked, again and again. There was a hero to be thanked and feted with free drinks. No one answered.

The Story

Room 372 was my dad's room here in the Kootenai Memorial Hospital Cancer Center. Sixty years of smoking had given him Stage 4 lung cancer, which had metastasized to his brain. The nebulizer that covered his nose, feeding oxygen to what was left of his lungs, made a repetitive clicking sound that signaled the delivery of air.

Mom and I sat at the foot of his bed, talking with him as best we could. He had to drop the nebulizer below his mouth in order to speak. The digital monitor on the unit displayed his oxygenation level, and whenever the level dropped below 88 percent, a shrill tone sounded. I thought the tone unnecessary as Dad always started gasping, unable to speak at 87 percent. Then he'd be forced to put the nebulizer back over his nose. We'd talk, and then I'd wait through his gasps while the machine recharged his blood with oxygen. It was painful to watch, worse to hear, but still I visited daily. You've probably heard the expression, "He looked like death warmed over." Now I'd seen it.

I'm Bob Evans. My father is Jack Evans, a retired Washington State Trooper. We never talked about his impending death, though we both knew it was coming. There was nothing to be gained by bringing it into our conversations. I privately prayed his death would come sooner than later. Sitting at the foot of his hospital bed I felt powerless, like I'd been disowned by my own balls.

"Son, I need to tell you about Mac," said Dad, when we were alone. "Listen now, this is not for your mother's ears. If she's here, Mac doesn't come up. If she walks in on us, we were talking about hamburgers. Nobody ever knew the truth. Here is what really happened." He was very serious, a fact he made clear by painfully forcing himself to sit up in bed. Wincing with every movement, he held eye contact with me for long seconds, even after the low-oxygen warning tone came on. Staring back at Dad, I realized I was holding my breath, depriving myself of oxygen just like he had by removing his nebulizer. Dad's quick gasping, at the pace of an exhausted runner's pant, made me want to flee the room.

"Okay, Dad, no problem. It'll be just between us."

"Mac and I grew up on the same street in Walla Walla and went to high school together. His dad died when he was 13. His mom was the nervous type. She worried a lot and was always wringing her hands. She had this shrill voice that was like listening to fingernails on a blackboard. Mac spent a lot of time at our house. Your grandparents weren't nervous or high strung, so they must have looked pretty good.

"When we were 14, Mac and I broke into a filling station. There we were, trying to pry open a cash box, when the cops showed up. I got away, but Mac didn't. He never told them that I was there, even when they offered to cut the sentence if he gave me up. They sent him to the state reform school in Chehalis for 15 months.

"We both enlisted in the Army on December 8, 1941, and went through basic training at Fort Ord, California. They called us 'Mac and Jack, the twins.' After basic we went to Fort Polk, Louisiana, for infantry training. Then he went on to a sniper school while I attended the military police school. Both happened to be at Fort McClelland in Anniston, Alabama."

I listened to Dad tell his story, watching the look in his eyes to see if he was back in the moment or here with me in the hospital room.

"After the training day ended we were free until the next morning. We'd go back to our different barracks, shit, shower and shave, and then meet up at the mess hall. We'd eat together, share news from home and then head out for beer. That was pretty much the way we spent most evenings. Our training school ran six days a week, Sundays off. Sunday morning most of the guys visited the sky pilot."

"What's a sky pilot?"

"That's the Chaplain. But Mac and I figured we needed to know our specialties a lot more than we needed to know God. We might be meeting him in person soon enough anyway."

"This was what, the middle of the summer of 1942?"

"Exactly! There was nothing but bad news coming from the Pacific and Europe. Hell, U-boats were sinking ships in the Gulf, just two hours south of Anniston. The whole country was scared shitless and wrapped tighter than bark on a tree. This was serious shit, but we couldn't wait to get in our own licks. The Krauts and the Japs were going to be shit-out-of-luck when Mac and Jack finally got into the fight."

"And you did it—you and Mac?"

Dad put the nebulizer back on and closed his eyes, taking in the largest breaths he could manage. Our silence was interrupted only by the soft mechanical pulse of the machine. Finally he opened his eyes, blinked and slid down the nebulizer. His voice was still that of a big man, deep, like a radio actor, even though his body had shrunk with age and become cadaverous from his long years of smoking.

"Mac and I were pretty serious about our training. We knew that we might not make it back, but by God we would take some of the bastards with us. In what little free time we had, we trained on our own. Mac practiced concealment, and he got really good at making these little screens. He'd cut branches and sort of weave them into a flat leafy mat that he could hide under. And Mac was a great shot. Anyway, he went off to a scout/sniper squad with the First Division."

"They called the First Division 'The Big Red One' didn't they?"

"That's right. You already know all about what I did during the war. He got back to the states in late 1945. Mac married his high school sweetheart and settled in Pullman. I had been accepted to be a state trooper by then, I'd married your mother and we bought the little house in Colfax where you grew up."

A coughing fit had interrupted his story. The flashing blue light of the digital monitor showed his oxygen level down to 85 percent. He fumbled to get the nebulizer back over his nose. I watched fearfully as he sucked air in rasping gasps. His eyes closed and his once-broad chest, now reduced to a boney cover for black lungs, twitched as he struggled for breath. He'd hit the wall.

"Dad, why don't you just lie back for a while and rest? I'll come back tomorrow, and you can tell me the rest of the story then." My throat thickened and my plea came out barely above a whisper. I couldn't watch any more suffering.

"No." The word came in a gasp.

"Really, I'll come back tomorrow when you're rested."

"No, listen now!" A hard stare bolstered the emphatic tone of his words.

"Okay, but why now?"

"Absolution."

I sat back in my chair with a nod, lifting my hands in an open-palms gesture, indicating he should go on.

"You remember how I brought my cruiser home? I was the resident trooper at Colfax. I patrolled a 100-mile circle that included Pullman. I'd stop and see Mac when I was in Pullman, or maybe we'd meet for coffee in Colfax if he was coming to town."

"I remember."

"We'd talk. He'd tell me about how the Pullman cops were riding his ass. Now, Mac always had a short fuse. He'd get tickets for double parking outside his appliance repair shop on Grand Avenue. Another time he told me about a bunch of run-ins he was having with a veteran who was at the college using the G.I. Bill. Henshaw, I think was his name. Who did what to whom first I don't know, but Mac was pissed. He said Henshaw had punched his wife when she was expecting and he thought it caused her to have a premature delivery."

21

Reaching the limit of his oxygen, he paused and raised the nebulizer to his nose. I looked away, not wanting to stare, until he spoke.

"Mac had this running war with Henshaw, but according to Mac, he was always the one who got charged with something. Anyway, on Easter Sunday, Mac brought his family up to our place in Colfax, and we went for a picnic on top of Steptoe Butte. You were just a baby then but you know the spot. They left for home about 3:00 in the afternoon. It must have been about 4:30 when I heard the squawk of the radio and then the call for assistance. You remember the big radio base station that I had in my den?"

"I do. You called it your 'business set' and how if I ever heard your call-sign, I should run and find you."

"That's right. Sheriff Purcell of Whitman County had just been killed. I was given the sniper's location so I'd know which way to approach. We were rolling units from Spokane, but they were more than an hour away, while I was only fifteen minutes out."

Another coughing fit stopped Dad from telling his story. He pulled up the nebulizer to cover his nose and inhaled as deeply as his wasted lungs would allow. I sat watching the monitors but didn't speak.

"God, I wish I had a smoke," he smiled. "When I arrived, everybody who was left had set up behind these two big steel grain elevators. Before the shooting there were only about ten law enforcement guys in the entire county. Now there were three cops dead and another wounded. The Pullman police chief at the time was an empty shirt, a blow-hard political hack. He had never been a cop and couldn't lead troops to free liquor. He got replaced by Archie Cameron, the senior surviving officer, soon after the massacre.

"Cameron filled me in. There was also a dead civilian and another citizen had been shot twice but was alive. They had the shooter holed up on this brushy hillside between the college

22

and the Palouse Highway. Then Archie told me the sniper's name."

Dad pulled up the nebulizer and inhaled. I looked out the window into a small courtyard and focused on the flowers and tried to identify them. Hydrangeas maybe? I turned back toward my father at the sound of his voice.

"The county prosecutor had put out a call for citizens to form a posse. I don't think any of them knew exactly what they were supposed to do, but they came anyway. Just then Mac took a shot at the Pullman police chief who was crouched down behind the fender of his car. The shot parts his hair and cut a clean line into his scalp, front to back. Blood ran down covering his entire face. An inch lower and his head would have exploded. He fell over backward and passed out. Mac must have been sorry he missed that shot. Anyway the chief came to and got helped to an ambulance.

Dad's recollections made him laugh, which brought on another coughing fit. On went the nebulizer and he tapped the button on his morphine drip as the nurse appeared in the doorway.

"Mr. Evans, are you doing all right? How about some ice chips?" Dad shook his head.

"I'll keep an eye on him," I said. "He just wants to finish telling me this story; we'll go slowly." She didn't smile back but stepped away with a shake of her head. Perhaps she knew that family time was the only thing her patient wanted this close to the end.

"After they hauled the Chief off, Cameron called us together and we stepped away from the posse.

"'Now, if any of you get the chance, shoot that son-of-a-bitch. He's already shot seven and killed four. He's got the high ground, cover, a sniper rifle and ammunition. We're putting all these students, farmers, and clerks in danger, but it's really up to us to get him. This ends here and now. Keep your people safe and let's put him down.'

23

"Mac wasn't coming off the hill alive. It was only a question of whether we could shoot him before he shot any more of us."

Another coughing fit overcame Dad. Getting up from my chair I raised the nebulizer mask to his nose and held it still in my hand until the fit subsided. When I tried to reach for the call button, Dad grabbed my wrist and shook his head in an emphatic 'no' gesture. His grip was strong as he squeezed my wrist, so I waited. When Dad finally began to speak, I took my seat.

"Archie divided the posse and the lawmen into four groups and told us what ways he wanted us to go. I was to lead eight men and a Moscow city cop around to the rear and try to approach Mac from the east. We piled into two cruisers and I led them up to a house on College Hill. We pulled behind a garage for cover. I told the Moscow cop I'd go scout, and that he and the others should find cover and set up a picket line below the garage.

"I moved away and started crawling along the ground headed to where we thought Mac was hiding. I was going really slow. The ground was as much sharp basalt chunks as it was dirt and I'd wince. I couldn't keep looking at the ground for fear of getting a stick in the eye from the snarl of brush that I had to crawl through. I kept calling out, 'Mac, its Jack, don't shoot me, I'm coming down.' I saw what I thought might have been one of Mac's woven mats of branches and called out again, 'Mac it's me, don't shoot.' He heard me and pushed himself up on his elbows.

Just then all hell broke loose, and I'm face down in the dirt and everybody was shooting from all sides. My face was literally in the dirt. I could turn to breathe but that was all. I hear bullets whizzing over my head and the gunfire sounded like the war. Leaves and dirt are getting kicked up and then I heard a bullet thump and Mac cry out.

"I honestly didn't know what I'd do when I got to Mac, but Cameron was right. There is a brotherhood of cops, and Mac had shot five of my brothers in blue. But he was my brother, too—just in a different way. What a Goddamn mess."

The oxygen generator beeped as Dad's oxygen level dropped to 87 percent. He put on the nebulizer mask, closed his eyes and began taking shallow breaths. I had to look away, wishing I was someplace other than there. Finally the beeping stopped and as I watched him, it was clear from the look in his eyes that was back there, reliving the scene.

"When the shooting stopped, I crawled over to where I'd seen Mac. I got to him and saw blood. Staying low myself, I helped him turn over. Someone from down below had managed to put a round into his chest. He was alive but hurt bad. We lay side by side in the quiet and I began to smell his blood, so I knew he was hit bad.

"'Mac, why the hell are you shooting people? Do you think you're back in the war? This is Pullman!

"'Aw, Jack. I just couldn't take any more of their shit. I tried complaining to the cops and the DA, but somehow it always ended up being my fault. Today on our way to your house, we stopped at the dairy for ice cream, and that asshole Henshaw was there. I pulled out a hunting knife and waved it at him, just to throw a scare into him so he'd leave us alone. We tussled, but I didn't cut him. I may have bitten him on the neck though.'

"'Mac, you're on probation from the last beef you had with Henshaw. You shouldn't have gotten into a brawl. You really bit him? Shit! Why didn't you tell me?'

"'When we got back to Pullman after the picnic, this city cop, Claar, came up to me at the gas station. He said he was going to arrest me, right there, for threatening Hershaw and violating my probation. He wasn't going to let me take my family home or anything. No slack. He knew my wife can't even drive. The son-of-a-bitch. When Claar went after his nightstick, it was just too much for me. I got my pistol from the glove box and shot him."

"'Christ, Mac, this is a mess. Listen, I'll get them to stop shooting. We'll get you patched up and find a good lawyer.' I stop talking as Mac lifts the palm of his hand up. His chest wound alternated bubbling red or sucking air, as he breathed.

"'It's too late, Jack. When I came up here, I knew that some cop was going to kill me today. Even if you take me down now, they'll still kill me. I'm done.'

"'No, you're not. I can help keep you safe and get you a lawyer. I'll look after your family. Hey, you're in the Chamber of Commerce, a sponsor for the Junior Chamber of Commerce and even a Scout leader. Not everybody likes the cops. You'll get sympathy and a good jury. I owe you. I've owed you since you took the rap for that gas station in Walla Walla. Now it's payback time and I'm ready to pay up.'

"'His breath was coming harder now and most of his shirt front had changed from green to red. 'You're right about one thing, brother, you do owe me. Here's what you owe,' and Mac paused to cough and tried to spit blood but just managed a trail of thick red drool from the corner of his mouth. 'I'm not going in. You'll do this for me.'

"'No way, absolutely not.' I knew what he wanted me to do. Then I paused, 'Why me?'

"'Because you're here. You're all I've got and you owe me. If you won't do it for me, at least give me your pistol. I can't manage with the rifle.'

"There were tears in his eyes as he gave me this big smile and jabbed at his chest with his index finger. He leaned back so I could be above him without getting shot myself. Mac kept tapping his chest, grinning that same shit-eating grin." Tears streaked Dad's face as his eyes closed and he slowly shook his head. After what seemed like minutes he fumbled for the nebulizer again. I waited for this hollow scarecrow who had been my dad to find his words.

"When it was done, I crawled back up the hill to the posse's picket line. I told the Moscow cop that I thought I'd found the sniper's nest and that he looked to be seriously wounded or dead. I waited with the posse while we radioed down to Cameron for instructions. He radioed back that he'd come up to me with the other cops who were down below. Then I led them back to Mac.

"We carried his body down the hill, hoisted above the brush that scratched and poked us as we passed, and laid him on the gravel by the railroad spur-line. People gathered in a half circle around Mac's body. One guy toed the body to make sure he was dead. I just couldn't take it." That said, Dad closed his damp eyes, and again we sat in silence for a few slowly dragging seconds. I was glad for the silence, my throat too thick to speak.

"I turned away from the group, slipped back across the tracks and sat down in the grass at the foot of the hill and cried. Finally, Cameron motioned for me to join him and we walked over to the silos for some privacy.

"'You shot him, didn't you?'

"I didn't answer.

"'Jack, let me see your gun.'

"Cameron opened the cylinder, saw the two cases with the firing pin marks, closed it and handed back my pistol. 'You'd be a hero. Why keep this a secret?'

"'Archie, I just helped kill my best friend. I'm ashamed of what I did, but I'd feel even worse if Mac had shot somebody else. There are no heroes here today, especially not me.'

"Understood."

"We walked back to the posse that surrounded Mac's body. I could smell all our sweat mixed with creosote from the rail ties, as the afternoon heat rose from rail bed and the gravel around the grain elevators. The posse quieted when Archie raised his arms for their attention.

"'Who thinks they got him?' Cameron asked everyone as they gathered around.

"'I think I did,' piped up some fella holding up a pistol. Archie didn't say anything, but he knew that was bull.

"'Anybody else think they got the sniper?' No one else spoke up. Cameron was still for a minute then spoke again.

27

'Who fired the last two shots?' and he looked at me. When I didn't speak, he did a slow turn, looking at each man. 'Well shit! I owe somebody a drink.' "

"Dad, are you still with me?" When I looked back at the bed he'd gone to sleep.

The call from the hospital woke my mom just after 8 a.m. the next day. Dad had passed during the night, she told me. I hoped he had passed quietly in his sleep and I was glad he died clean, in a hospital, not like Mac. I remember him as a soldier and a trooper, who, no matter how hard, would always do what needed to be done.

Epilogue

Neither the Whitman County prosecutor nor the coroner has ever talked about the Easter Massacre, even 66 years later. The Whitman County Historical Society shared what information they held. There was no autopsy report on McIntyre's body. In an interview, the doctor who examined McIntyre's body said three bullets, all fired from the same angle, had pierced his chest. The angle and the close grouping of the shots were a puzzle. The doctor, prosecutor and law enforcement all agreed that only a fully automatic weapon could fire quickly enough to put three holes in such a tight group. They felt that some former soldier, on campus using his G.I. bill, had brought back a .30 caliber carbine and used it to shoot McIntyre. Their theory was that because the possession of such an automatic weapon was illegal, the shooter chose to remain anonymous.

I held both the bullets that were removed from McIntyre's rifle, and the slugs removed from the bodies of Deputy Gallagher, Ernest Buck and George McIntyre. Could an analysis of the bullets that killed McIntyre have been matched to a gun? Perhaps, but no such comparisons were ever attempted.

Who shot McIntyre? According to the records, no one knows and no one wants to find out. It was just someone who stepped up and was willing to do what needed to be done.

The End

Author's Notes

The Easter Massacre story was told to me by a member of the 1949 posse. The only fictionalized part of the story is, who shot George McIntyre?

The material in the Prologue and Epilogue is from newspaper accounts, Whitman County agencies and the Whitman County Historical Society. The names of the actual participants are used in these sections. In the fictional answer to the question of who shot George McIntyre, some names have been changed.

3. The Grand Tetons

It was a hot August day in 1969 when Janet Lee walked into the center of Clarksville, Texas from where she parked her car in the Seven Eleven lot by the highway. Her home town in Oklahoma looked just like this one. The square of every small Texas town had either a courthouse or a city hall on one side. Across the square was the bank, and between the two, in the center of the square, was a flagpole with a cannon at its base. The red, white and blue of the Texas flag hung just below Old Glory. With no breeze, the two flags blended into one mass of colors.

"I wonder if this is the Clarksville that The Monkees sang about?" she muttered as she crossed the square. The Walmart that had come to town last year had already driven out many of the local merchants. The storefronts on the square were all empty except for the Farmers and Merchants Bank. That was all she needed. It was more than that. It was a gift, and you could make more of it.

Entering the bank, Janet let her eyes adjust to the interior lighting. A manager sat at a desk in the rear of the lobby. She doodled on a withdrawal slip before taking it over to the lone teller who stood at one of the three stations.

"Hello." She switched on her most dazzling smile, tossed her ash-blond hair and beamed at the young man with her bright blue eyes.

"Good morning Ma'am." He flushed. "Ar...eh...I mean good afternoon." He finally managed to get out, "How can I help you today?"

"Well thank you." She smiled and passed the withdrawal slip across the counter. "I'd like to make a withdrawal, please."

Slowly she opened the front of her short denim jacket, first one side and then the other, to reveal the white fishnet of her tank top. The smile on the face of the young man disappeared. His eyes were drawn to the rose-pink nipples that seemed to be staring at him through the mesh. He tried looking back up to her brilliant smile but couldn't. From her round, firm breasts the rosy nipples were still staring up at his eyes. Then his gaze dropped to the large brown wood gun butt that hugged the flat of her stomach. Some emblem, a Texas star perhaps, was inset on the grip.

"Take all the money from your drawer and put it in the bag, honey." She held eye contact with him, even though his stare had not yet left the gun. She removed a white flour sack from her back pocket and passed it across the counter. "Please don't spoil either of our days by pushing any alarm. Momma needs the money for her surgery, and I'm just trying to be a good daughter."

When the full bag slid back across the counter, she spoke again. "Wait just a bit before you do anything." She did her best to portray both innocence and vulnerability by managing a small frown. Then, buttoning the middle button on her jacket, she walked out of the bank, but not out of his dreams.

* * *

"So can you tell me what she was wearing?" asked the Deputy Sheriff Muldrow, from Red River County.

"Denim jeans and a denim jacket," was the response. The answer from the teller started the deputy writing in his notebook as they sat across the table in the bank's employee lounge.

"What color was her hair?"

"I don't remember." The teller stared at the table, avoiding eye contact with the deputy.

"What about the color of her eyes?"

"I don't remember." The deputy pressed on.

"Did she have a gun?"

"Yes, there was a gun."

At last they we're back on track. "Okay, what kind of a gun was it?"

"Big gun." He shook his head apologetically.

Trying not to let his frustration show, the deputy tried again. "Is there anything else you can recall?" The teller didn't seem to hear the question. After what seemed like a minute, Muldrow repeated the question.

"She had a beautiful smile. I just couldn't seem to tear my eyes away."

"From her smile?"

"Yes that's right, from her smile." Then he shut up. He wasn't about to volunteer that all he could recall were her beautiful breasts.

* * *

Janet Lee Durham sat in her yard swing back home in Idabel, Oklahoma, and counted the money from the Clarksville bank: $1,562. Checking that no one was around, she tucked the bills into her tank top and went back into the house. Fishing the loot out from her cleavage, she added it to the dollars already in a bag balm tin hidden in the bottom of her underwear drawer.

Janet Lee was the only daughter of Ray and Thelma Mahoney and had grown up in Idabel. She'd learned to fight from her three brothers, but she'd learned to drink bourbon— with a beer back—from her father. She'd learned how to handle a gun in the military police.

Most important to her recent success was what she had learned about men. It had been a long tutorial that started in the back seat of a Pontiac convertible during high school. Men who found her irresistible were easily led. They would follow her anywhere if, either literally or figuratively, she had ahold of their dicks.

Better still, all she really had to do was make men want her. Beyond being smart, confident and beautiful, Janet Lee Durham was tough. She was well armed with the big Colt revolver her father had given her when she graduated from the Military Police School at Fort McClelland, Alabama, and just as lethal...with her irresistible sex appeal.

* * *

De Kalb, Texas, was in Bowie County, 25 miles east of Clarksville. Janet Lee figured that the sheriffs in the two adjacent counties wouldn't be expecting another robbery so soon after the Clarksville job.

Three days after Clarksville, Janet Lee pulled into DeKalb. She passed the Walmart on the way in and parked one block off the town square. The scene was only different because this county courthouse was built out of red sandstone instead of brick. The one-time bank building was now home to the Red River Army Depot Credit Union. Crossing the street past the obligatory cannon, she stopped to look down the muzzle. An empty Dr. Pepper can peered back with its cyclops-like pop-top eye.

"Well, you are real at least." She gave the cannon barrel a pat. "I was wondering if they got a bulk price on you guys from Cannons 'R' Us." From the cannon, Janet Lee had a clear view inside the credit union, right through its large, plate-glass windows. The lobby was empty like the storefronts that ringed the square.

Today she had dressed in tight brown slacks, a matching waist-length jacket, boots and a white cowboy hat. She wore large gold hoop earrings. Looking good and feeling better, she strode into the lobby of the credit union. Stopping to pretend to write out a deposit slip gave her a moment to study the lobby and decide if there was a suitable teller she could target. There was.

"Hello, may I help you?" The middle-aged teller's hair was receding at the temples, with gray starting to appear. Janet Lee smiled back as she slowly opened her jacket. His glasses slid down his nose as he lowered his gaze to her chest. Her breasts strained the mesh of her fishnet top, one nipple peeking proudly out while the other strained enticingly against the mesh. She detected the brief move of his eyes from her chest to the gun butt showing above her silver and gold belt buckle.

"You're cute, mister," Janet Lee said with a smile. "Please don't spoil this day for either of us. I'll be gone in one minute, and I need the money for my tuition. Please put the cash from your drawer right into this bag," and she passed the same flour sack to him.

He emptied the contents of his drawer into her bag and passed it back. She also removed one of his business cards from the card rack on the counter.

"John Stevens, it's been a pleasure doing business with you. Please keep this transaction our little secret for, say... five minutes. If you do that for me, I won't come calling at your house." She waved his card in her fingers. Buttoning the middle button of her jacket, she turned and left. John Stevens silently watched her go. When fully out of his trance, he walked briskly from the teller cages to the desk of his manager.

"Mr. Majeski, I just got robbed."

* * *

The day after the robbery, John was seated at the table in the staff break room, a glass of water in his hand, when the manager came in with the one and only DeKalb City Police detective.

"John, I'm Detective Lambert. Getting robbed is pretty upsetting isn't it?" John didn't look up from his water glass, but nodded in agreement. Lambert took a seat across the table.

"I'd like you to tell me what you can about the robbery. What did the robber look like? What was said? Was there a note presented? Did you see a gun? Just tell me what you can,"

"I'll leave you two alone," said the branch manager and left the room. Stevens and Lambert sat silently for several minutes.

Finally, the detective broke the silence. "Listen, you didn't do anything wrong, here. Nobody is unhappy with you. The money is insured and no one got hurt; that's what counts. How about you begin with when you first saw the robber. Just start talking and we'll sort out what I need."

"She was young and very blond. Nicely dressed in a western-cut suit... and she wore a white Stetson."

"What color were her eyes?"

"I didn't notice." This was a lie that couldn't be challenged.

"Can you guess her height or weight? Was her build slim, medium, or heavy?"

"Honestly, once I saw her," and John paused—a long pause—before continuing. "When I saw her gun...after that I didn't pay too much attention to what she looked like. All I could see was her..." He paused again, swallowing, "...gun."

"That's okay John; guns are pretty unnerving. Did she point it at you?"

"Ah no, she just opened her jacket and showed me what she had." He thought it would be safer to lie by omission. He preferred emphasizing the rise in his blood pressure caused by Janet's opening her jacket, and didn't mention the rise in his pants.

"Anything else you can remember? How about the gun? Was it a revolver or an automatic? Was it black or nickel?"

"Sorry, all that I can say is that what I saw looked big. I'll never forget what I saw if I live to be a hundred. I relive that image whenever I close my eyes."

* * *

Janet Lee Durham had only one heart's desire when she began robbing banks. She wanted to trade off her shit-box Ford pickup and get the 'Judge' model, 1969 Pontiac GTO. What girl wouldn't be seduced by the orange car featured in the Pontiac ad campaign? She longed to feel the leather bucket seats caressing her back. She could imagine the vibrating power of those 389 cubic inches rushing up through her feet to her thighs. After two bank jobs she was half way to the $6,759 she needed for the car.

Janet Lee worked a day job as a waitress in the restaurant her husband managed. Her earning and tips, along with the robbery money—which she had failed to mention to her husband, Jimmy—were all being saved for the car.

"Please God, just this one little thing, and I'll retire from crime and never sin again." Not wanting to lie to God, she quickly amended her prayer. "Well, at least I'll retire from crime." She didn't know if one could pray for God's help in committing a felony, but there seemed to be no harm in asking. It was kind of like dating, she figured; if you never asked, you never got a "yes."

"Baby, that GTO will be the most fun we can have with our clothes on," she told Jimmy when he asked about how her car funding was coming along.

* * *

George Oostergard was the lone FBI agent stationed in Texarkana, Texas. His office was in the federal courthouse at the east end of State Line Boulevard, straddling the Texas and Arkansas border. This allowed the Eastern District of Texas and the Western District of Arkansas to share courtroom space in the same building.

Once a month he attended a Tri-County Investigators meeting. Police and sheriff's detectives from Red River and

Bowie counties met with their counterparts from Miller County, Arkansas. Each agency shared details about their ongoing investigations and recent crimes. The meeting usually lasted an hour before the group adjourned for an executive session at Fat Jack's bar.

The Clarksville and DeKalb robberies had both happened within the past ten days. The FBI had jurisdiction over crimes involving federally insured banks and credit unions if the locals chose not to pursue matters under their own state laws. George had not been invited in on either case, perhaps because of the thinly veiled local suspicion of all things federal. The 1865 surrender at Appomattox had ended the fighting but not the distrust between the North and South. Beer or bourbon consumed face to face with colleagues was all they had to break through the institutional suspicions.

Deputy Rick Muldrow from the Red River County Sheriff's Department was having a drink with Detective Skip Lambert from DeKalb PD. Seeing George enter the bar, Muldrow motioned for the FBI Agent to join them.

"George, why is it that you take lots of notes at our meeting, but when it's your turn to speak, you never say shit? Not a damn word." Muldrow's delivered the comment as a friendly ribbing. For the FBI, sharing information was a one-way street.

George could only shake his head. "Fellas, I'm just trying to learn from the real pros. Besides, you know you'd never listen to whatever I had to say anyway. Now which one of you assholes—I mean gentlemen—is going to buy me a beer?"

It was during the second beer that Skip Lambert heard a surprising similarity between his victim at the DeKalb credit union robbery and Rick Muldrow's reluctant bank teller in Clarksville. Skip shared his skepticism about the perception or memory lapses of his victim.

George's curiosity was piqued.

"Would you mind if I had a chat with your victims?" He steepled his fingers. "It does sound like they didn't give up the full story. I wonder why? If I find out anything more, it's yours

37

to use." Oostergard nodded at one then the other of his companions. "At the very least, I can issue and circulate a Crime Alert Bulletin in East Texas and Western Arkansas to all of our officers and the local departments."

"Knock yourself out, George." Detective Lambert leaned back from their table.

"Rick?" Agent Oostergard waited.

"Sure," Muldrow nodded.

* * *

Agent Oostergard arranged for meetings with the two tellers. Each interview took place at the office of the local lead investigator. Lambert and Muldrow observed from out of sight as George interviewed the tellers. He chose to interview Terry Grunsberg, the 21-year-old from Clarksville first. His answers had been the most suspicious, and being younger, he should be easier to break in an interview.

"Terry thanks for coming in today. I'm FBI Special Agent George Oostergard. I'm interested in the robbery because bank robbery is a federal crime. So let me start by going over Deputy Muldrow's notes from his interview. Tell me if anything got left out," and Oostergard read back the interview portion of the crime report provided by the deputy.

"Did we miss anything?

The teller stopped, sipped from a Dr. Pepper and signaled with a shake of his head that nothing had been missed.

"Terry, I've been an agent for more than twenty years. I've got to say that your statement—well son, it didn't pass my personal stink test. So you and I are going to start over with a clean sheet. Now, this is important. I want you to think back to the robbery." Adding emphasis, George slowed his speech and hit on each of the next five words separately. "Give me every little detail."

"Here's the thing; this is now a federal crime. You seem to be a fine young man. I'm sure that your folks are real proud of you. You're making a good start in the working world there at the bank. So I don't want to find out that the reason you're holding back information is because you knew the robber or were in on the plan somehow. That would derail all the good things you've got going. Now, let's get started."

Terry feared pissing off the FBI more than he feared embarrassment. He spilled the whole story about the hot lady bank robber. The teller was now able to describe, in—minute detail—the bank robber's wardrobe, hair color and skin tone. It appeared that once he started talking, he couldn't stop, even venturing so far as to offer a guess about her cup size.

Armed with this new information, Agent Oostergard re-interviewed John Stevens, using the same set-up scenario that had successfully motivated Grunsberg. Then the agent revealed his hole-card.

"I understand that besides looking like every man's wet-dream of a rodeo queen, she made a point of showing you her great knockers. 34-DD's would you say?"

Stevens sighed and they began. An hour later, every detail had been revealed. John clung to his claim that he'd been threatened, and that was why he'd withheld the details.

Acting upon what now appeared to be a distinctive crime signature and with more complete information, the bureau sent a Crime Alert Bulletin to all local and federal law enforcement offices in Arkansas, Oklahoma and Texas. At this point, the prosecuting attorneys for the two Texas counties were only too happy to turn over their cases to the federal government. Soon after, a federal grand jury returned a two-count indictment against a Jane Doe. Janet Lee Durham was now a wanted federal fugitive. Fortunately for the feds, she didn't know about the Crime Bulletin when she hit the bank in Paris, Texas.

* * *

39

The Cattleman's Bank and Trust had the FBI Crime Alert flyer posted in its break room. Since surveillance camera technology had not yet arrived on the bank security scene, the flyer had only a composite sketch of the robber. When Janet showed what was under her coat this time, the young man immediately hit a silent alarm. He then turned and asked the head teller, Mrs. Dorothy Jones, to help him at the window. Dorothy took one look at the young robber and smiled.

"Oh honey, you can put those away. You probably have about another ninety seconds before the cops arrive. I'd be going if I were you."

Janet got only as far as the front door before the first police car arrived. She didn't resist the two officers with drawn guns. When she raised her hands as instructed, all of her weapons were revealed. Sitting behind the cage in the back of the police car, now unarmed, she heard one of the officers in the front seat whistle and say, "Nice tits."

"Yes they are. Eat your heart out."

Looking out through the bars of the patrol car, she glimpsed a GTO, its sleek body gleaming orange, its windows winking in the sunlight. She heard the motor purr and watched as her orange wet dream vanished.

The End

Author's Notes

The Grand Tetons is based on robberies that took place in Baldwin Park, California and during my subsequent parole supervision in north Idaho. The Texas and Arkansas settings are based on where I was stationed for part of the first Gulf War, after being called back to active duty and away from my posting in Idaho.

4. The Happy Endings Retirement Home

Janet Lee Durham was sentenced to five years by the federal court for armed bank robbery. She made good use of her time in prison, taking classes to become a Certified Nurse's Assistant.

Her classmates were the Tinderia twins, Arleen and Darleen. They were identical twins, but Arleen had developed a greater love for pasta than her sister. The twins were co-defendants, each serving five-year bits for tax evasion and the attempted bribery of a federal judge.

Born and raised in Elko, Nevada, the twins had successfully operated Mabel's, a brothel on Third Street just behind Stockman's Casino. The two sisters took a motherly interest in their young Texas friend. Initially, the three bonded over their shared love of fast cars. The twins favored Fords, and each year they used to buy a new pair of identical Mustangs. Janet preferred the American iron from General Motors.

"We used to call Mustangs 'pony cars.' Now we call them 'ass-holes' because everybody's got one," mused Darleen. "We get something different every year now. Honestly Janet, if it's got a dick or a stick, Arleen's been for a ride," confided Darlene.

Arleen just smiled. "I can't help it if I'm irresistible to men. They like a big, complete girl, soft like a feather pillow. No sharp points or edges, if you know what I mean."

"So tell me about your case." Janet leaned her elbows on the prison cafeteria table. 'I've already run you through my tale of woe. What about you two?'"

"Do you want to tell it, Arleen?"

"No, you go right ahead. I'll chime in if you leave anything out."

"A brothel is a wonderful business. Non-polluting, uses a renewable resource and it's an entry level spot in the job market for women."

41

"And it's a cash business, mostly," Arleen interjected, putting her hand on Janet's wrist.

"Anyway, all was well for nearly twenty years… until we crossed paths with the Judge. He was something of a regular every few months."

Arleen leaned forward to get another word in.

"He liked more experienced talents, like me. So for him, I'd come out of management and occasionally dabble in customer service. Darleen was known for her good head for business. I was just known for good head. Well anyway, he was a nice enough old goat, but then he started wanting discounts. I told him that Mabel's wasn't a Holiday Inn, where you stay ten nights and get the next one free."

"So when Arleen told him that free wasn't an option, he pulled the 'Judge card' as they say," Darleen interrupted.

"Didn't you try to bribe him?"

"Sure we did, but then he demanded more. He wanted a free pass to all the girls… and cash! Can you imagine the balls on that guy?"

"I can," replied Arleen.

Darleen picked up the story. "The Judge put the IRS onto us."

"How did they ever prove tax evasion? Isn't that a cash business? The customers pay the girls in private, right? So how did they prove the skim?"

The twins looked at each other, before Darleen answered. "They clocked the visitors coming in the front and counted the dirty towels going out the back. They figured one towel per visitor and an average charge of fifty bucks."

"Smart, but what about the bribery?"

"That was her idea," Darleen said, nodding towards Arleen.

"I managed to get a meeting, in-chambers, with the judge and the two attorneys. There we were, just the four of us. I said that I had a female emergency and asked to use the bathroom in-chambers. What man is going to argue with a female emergency? So I went in and stayed there. Finally, the Judge sent the two attorneys out of his chambers. He told them he'd call when I finally came out. Then he knocked and came in. That's when I offered the bribe. I said I'd put him on the blow-jobs-for life plan. I gave the old goat a free sample and even took my teeth out."

"Tell her what happened next, Arleen."

"We go back into chambers. He called the attorneys back and told them that I had tried to extort him and had offered him a bribe."

"In the end, we cut a deal to get the extortion count dropped and plead to the attempted bribery and tax evasion. Talk about crime, now that was a crime," Darleen said, as she shook her head in an, 'Oh well' gesture.

"So Janet, what are you going to do when you parole?" asked Arleen.

"I can't go home to Idabel. Too many folks know about my crimes. Returning there would complicate things for my parents. They sure don't need any more grief. And my husband Jimmy, he's had it with me. I think I'll go back to Killeen, Texas, just outside Fort Hood. It was my duty station where I was an MP. And where will the two of you go? Back to Elko?"

"Absolutely. Elko is our home."

* * *

After 3 years served, Janet paroled to Killeen, Texas. Being a certified CNA made it easy for her to find a job at the Happy Years retirement home. Still young, strong and friendly, she was well received by the patients and staff. Her conviction did not cancel her G.I. Bill benefits and Janet continued her education. Within two years she acquired her Licensed Vocational Nursing certification. Continuing at the local college, a Bachelor of Science in Hospital Administration was her next target. The degree took her three years of night and summer classes, but she made it.

* * *

22 Apr, 78
Dear Arleen,

I hope you and Darleen are both well. I just graduated from West Texas State with my degree in hospital administration. That means I could be buying the bedpans instead of emptying them.

I've got a plan for my future, but I need help from you girls, if you're interested and able. I want to buy the retirement home where I'm working. As they say, 'I've learned the business from the bottom up.' Actually I've learned it from many bottoms. I've investigated the Texas licensing requirements.

Being a felon, I cannot be granted a license, but I can work in the business in any other capacity. I'll be the manager and I'd like you two to be my shift supervisors. I have a woman from my YWCA class who can get a license. I helped her get out of an abusive relationship with a mean drunk of a husband. She'll get a license and show up whenever needed, but otherwise she wants nothing in return. I have two other older ladies who've aged out of the escort business. They are willing to work for room, board and a small salary.

What I need from you girls is financing and reliable partners. If you and Darleen have any interest in my proposal, let's talk.

My last question for you is this. If two high school sweethearts from Elko get married and twenty-years later get divorced, are they still cousins?
Janet

44

May 10, 1978
Dear Janet,

We love your idea and think we can contribute more than money. And yes, the divorced couple would still be cousins, unless of course they were brother and sister to start.

Elko has gone straight to hell. The old cowboy casinos, Commercial Hotel and Stockman's are still here, but the town has gone Vegas. There is a new strip with a big Red Lion hotel and casino. It's all big money chains, neon, fast food and gas stations now. The cowboy soul of Elko has left town and been replaced by tract homes for the miners at Carlin. Our convictions keep us from getting back into the business, even if we wanted to. A change of scenery would be nice. Frankly, we're tired of just sitting around feeding the black-tail deer at our little ranch out here in Starr Valley.

Darleen suggests that we tailor our marketing plan toward older men. Maybe change the name of the place from The Happy Years to The Happy Endings. We'll have happy customers and a waiting list for admissions. With our experience, we'll give the best bed baths in town. We thought of having a French Day every week. You know, french toast for breakfast, french fries and french dip for lunch, and a special french treat for the fellas to liven things up in the afternoon. There will also be a Hawaiian night. We'll serve Kahlua Pig or some such and all the residents will receive nice lei. I'm sure that between us we'll be able to come up with other ways to keep our customers satisfied. Maybe Greek night, but I'll have to talk to the girls. About the money, no problem, just let us know what you need.
Love,
Arleen

* * *

Darleen and Arleen joined Janet in Texas. They bought The Happy Years Retirement Home and renamed it, The Happy Endings Retirement Home. Using Darleen's business plan, the venture thrived. They had no complaints from their very satisfied male customers. Like the twins had predicted, men were lining up to enjoy many happy endings with the girls. Advertised quietly by word of mouth, they soon needed a waiting list.

Janet did the hiring of professional staff. Women who had previously been victims found shelter, work and self-confidence working at the Happy Endings. When her employees aged out of dealing with their gentlemen, they became cooks or housekeepers. She arranged for them to share free rooms in a small house nearby. No woman was ever put out on the street or forced back to an abusive husband.

The twins did the hiring for the comfort care staff. They had perfected their own set of qualifications. They knew from their days running Mabel's that some workers developed a deep and abiding hatred for men. Other girls loved men, loved sex and loved the power they achieved by gently controlling the sexual experience. Arleen and Darleen also had learned to size up potential customers. Widowers made excellent residents, as did men who grew up with older sisters. They had few problems with residents misbehaving.

The special services that The Happy Endings provided were also presented as rewards, not rights. This distinction was soon made apparent to any new guests that misbehaved. Like any football or hockey team, the twins had a designated enforcer. Miss Begonia, the Fudge Hammer.

Begonia Thibedaux got the Fudge Hammer moniker because she was oh, so sweet, but hit so hard. Her five-foot-one, 210-pound body looked much like a bowling ball, except when she wore the tubular spandex she favored. As she often told men during her professional days, "Honey, I'm built for comfort, not for speed."

Today, Begonia had an assignment; provide a come-to-Jesus moment for Mr. Joe Bob White. She had been warned about Joe Bob's bad habit and knew what to expect during his bed bath.

Joe Bob stiffened as he lay there. The warm, wet cloth in Begonia's hand was hitting all the right spots. He could feel his own happy ending approaching. That was when he grabbed her bare shoulder and pulled her down. Begonia's response was swift. She hit him right as his spray hit her. Pow! Her fist connected with his jaw. Joe Bob's eyes vibrated. She yanked the towel up from the bed and wiped the white splatter from her cheek.

"Don't you be gettin' that sticky stuff on me!" She grabbed his scrotum with her left hand and squeezed the wrinkled sack. Joe Bob's breath blew out through his nose and mouth in one giant rush.

"If you want the rub, don't be messin' with the lady, bub! You feel me honey? You are here for what we can give, not what you can take." Begonia began nodding, all the time squeezing with her left hand. The prostrate figure, with eyes bugged out, finally managed a nod of agreement, signaling profound understanding. She released her grip and retrieved the towel she had brought to the bed.

"I'm gonna come visit you tomorrow, honey. If you behave yourself, we'll get along fine and your regular lady can come back after that. You feel me?"

"Yes."

"That's better, baby." Patting his cheek with an open right hand, Begonia smiled and left.

* * *

Besides her shift work at The Happy Endings, Janet volunteered at the local YWCA. Three times each year, she taught a women's self-defense class, using the skills she had

47

acquired in the Army. Janet was passionate about empowering women. Too many of her students had been the victims of abuse by husbands, boyfriends, fathers or brothers. Janet wanted to rebuild or instill in her students a sense of power, dignity and confidence that had been destroyed by men.

"Watch and learn, ladies." Janet faced her class. She wore a pink T-shirt with the image of Wonder Woman stenciled across the front. Ringing the image were the words, "Fight like a Girl." One-on-one, she allowed her students to learn skills by using them, first on her, and then on a female partner, until the needed muscle memory became ingrained. Gradually, her students found their power and began to regain confidence and self-esteem. She savored the visible increases in confidence among her students.

"So, to escape being choked, you just lower your head quickly and step back. Then run like hell. Now, watch how I get out of a headlock. Okay Ruby, will you help me demonstrate?"

Ruby George stepped out into the circle of women.

"Put me in a good tight headlock, okay?" Janet gave a grunt as Ruby swung her arm around the instructor's head. "Watch, ladies. I'm going to put my hands on her elbow and her shoulder, then push, and I'm free. Then what ladies?"

"Run like hell!" they all chimed in enthusiastically.

The last class always ended the same way. "The size of your abuser doesn't matter. What does matter is that you find calm within yourself. Only focus on one thing at a time, no matter how loud, chaotic or desperate the situation gets. Sometimes you may not be able to get free and get away. Texas law spells out the lawful uses of deadly force. Deadly force is legal in defense of your own life, or in defense of the life of another, like your child. So," and she paused for emphasis, "you were in fear for your life or your child's life when you defended yourself. Do you all understand?" No one spoke. "Let me say it again. If you use anything close to deadly force, you were in fear for your life." She said each word slowly and with emphasis, making eye contact with each student as she spoke. Then, feeling she had made her point, she moved on.

"So, who thinks they know the shortest way to a man's heart? Anyone?"

"Through his stomach, is what they say," responded Ruby.

"Any other guesses?"

"Under his stomach," smiled Marla, causing a titter to move among the class.

"Actually ladies, the shortest way to a man's heart is between his fourth and fifth ribs.

"Remember, your first and best move is to get away if you can. Don't be afraid to run. Just take the kids and go. You do have options. You do have friends. There are safe places, like here at the YWCA, the police station, the hospital, or call me. God bless yawl, you've been a great group."

* * *

Janet was having her regular weekly lunch meeting with the twins at Luby's Cafeteria. Harley George had tracked Janet from the YWCA, just like he had tracked his girlfriend Ruby to Janet's self-defense class. He'd find out who was responsible for giving his lady the nerve to leave him.

"I'm going to get the bitch that made Ruby forget her place. Then I'll deal with Ruby. That shit just won't fly." He pounded his fist on the bar at the Stars and Bars Tavern.

Outside the Happy Endings he had seen Janet and the twins drive away as he pulled up. He followed them to Luby's. Inside his Ford Ranger, George worked the slides on two automatic pistols, chambering the 9mm rounds. He touched his pants pockets to make sure the extra magazines for the pistols were still there.

"Let's get her done." He started the engine, pointed the Ford toward Luby's, and drove right through a plate glass window

49

into the front of the restaurant. He walked over broken glass, spilled food and shattered booths, and found Janet in the chaos. Stunned by the noise from the truck, the explosion of glass, and the screams of the patrons, the twins had momentarily frozen in place. Janet was busy pushing them under the table when George approached and then stopped.

"This is for what you've done to me and my Ruby. This is payback day!"

Janet didn't need to think. She found calm within herself and focused only on one thing in the chaos of the moment.

"Hello handsome," she smiled. Stepping into the armed man, she reached for his right wrist, hoping for the chance to disarm him like she knew she could.

"Bitch!" George shot her twice, then twice more. Janet died amid the broken dishes and spilled food.

For ten minutes, George stalked through the restaurant selecting women to shoot. He killed 23 and wounded another 27. When the police arrived, a wounded George retreated to a bathroom and did the right thing, shooting himself in the head.

Ten of his victims were killed with one shot to the head. The detectives later commented that among the victims, these ten women most resembled George's mother.

When Luby's reopened five months later, they began a policy of giving a 25 percent discount to any armed law enforcement officer that came through their doors. Luby's closed its doors for the final time in September 2000. Gone, but not forgotten.

The End

Author's Notes

The Texas and Arkansas settings are based on where I was stationed for part of the first Gulf War in 1990-91. The Tinderia sisters are based on a professional escort I supervised after her conviction for tax evasion. The judge's behavior is based on her description of a true encounter. Begonia is based on a local tribal member I supervised. She had a similar shape and strength. The Luby's massacre happened while I was on temporary assignment with the Army CID at Fort Hood, Texas.

5. Pinky and the Piper

With their prison industries jobs done for the day, the old con and his two young acolytes returned to the prison yard during free recreation. The yard, an expanse of asphalt inside a double row of eight-foot-high wire fences, ringed with spirals of razor wire, stretched from the main building wall to the water's edge. Fast Eddie Briggs was holding court in the yard. There at his feet, as befitted his criminal royalty, were Jack 'Scotty' Barker and Raymond 'Pinky' Bowles.

Eddie's butt was planted on the top of the picnic table, putting his knees at the level of the two young men who sat on the bench. Jack and Ray were first-time bank robbers. Eddie, on the other hand, had made a career of robbing banks. As a famous predecessor had said, "That's where the money is."

The three were dressed like triplets in khaki colored pants and shirts and black oxfords. Their denim jackets protected them against the wind that blew in across the Long Beach Harbor. Had there been insignias of rank on their shirts, they might have been at March Air Force Base. But this was the yard at the Federal Correctional Institution, Terminal Island, California. Nice, as federal correction facilities go, but certainly not a 'Club Fed,' as inmates called the camp facilities of the Bureau of Prisons. There were no prison walls or guard towers here, just wire-topped fences and unarmed correctional staff supervising the yard. Still, no one thought for a second that they were free.

"Now pay attention, my little grasshoppers," directed Eddie. "Here are the Eddie Briggs rules for success. Take them or leave them, but know I've probably robbed more banks than the two of you ever walked into."

The two young cons leaned closer.

"Rule one," Eddie said, pointing an index finger and thumb in their direction. "Fit in. Don't look like a bank robber. You want to look respectable. You want to blend in with your surroundings."

The two looked at each other before one thought to ask, "Like what?"

"Simple; if the bank is in downtown San Francisco, you should be in a jacket and tie. But if you're robbing the bank in East Jesus, Idaho, you should be dressed like, I don't know, a logger or cowboy or whatever. Look like you belong there, stupid.

"Rule two. Never take a gun. You might be tempted to use it. Pulling a gun can only get somebody shot, and it just might be you. Besides, having a gun in the commission of a federal bank robbery is an automatic five-year sentence bump. It is, however, okay to say you have a gun.

"Rule three. Forget everything you ever saw on TV or the movies about a bank job. It isn't like that. For instance, don't be going in and casing the place. You're a stranger there, and you'll be remembered. Assume that small town banks have cameras, but no guards or dye packs in the money. Big city banks, on the other hand, have off-duty cops as tellers, and a lobby guard besides.

"Rule four. Don't do what the cops expect you to do. Don't speed away in a stolen car with out-of-state plates. Don't run out of the bank; walk. Know where you're going to go and how you'll get there.

"Rule Five. Don't try to get into the vault. Vault heists are movie shit. It's safer to think small and be satisfied with one teller's drawer, which usually has about three grand. Tellers keep their stash of big bills, the fifties and hundreds, in separate envelopes inside their drawers. So don't get away without those.

"Rule Six. Don't wear masks that you have to put on outside the bank and then take off. Disguise your appearance. Grow facial hair you can shave off." Eddie pantomimed stroking a beard. "Wear a wig to change your hair color. Use an eyebrow pencil to draw a removable tattoo on your neck. Use pancake make-up to change your skin tone. Buy two pair of boots at Goodwill. Rip the soles off one pair and glue them to the soles of the other pair. Then put lifts inside that pair so you've changed your height by a good two inches without being obvious."

Eddie went silent, while he looked over the heads of the two young cons and out across the harbor. Ray rubbed the pink burn scars on his hands then decided to look where Eddie was looking. Seeing nothing, he turned to Jack, winked and said, "This is good stuff." Then he turned back to Eddie. "Ah, Eddie, is there anything else?"

"I was thinking about my days in the Navy, at the end of the second war. There was a bar over there, Joe Biff's Tavern. We'd go there on liberty. Half the time we'd end up in a brawl—it was great!"

Eddie's focus was far from the prison and the two young cons. Jack smiled at Ray, rolling his eyes. Ray and Jack had spent the last year in the same cell house with Eddie. For them, Eddie was like their aging uncle, trying his best to help his young nephews. They knew that sometimes poor old Eddie got stuck in time. Right now he was a full thirty years back to 1945 and no longer with them in 1975. They would get nothing more from him today.

"Listen you two; I'll save the rest for another time. I think your brains are full for today." With that Eddie raised himself from the table top and walked over to the perimeter fence. Jack and Ray drifted off, leaving the old con staring out across the water toward Joe Biff's.

* * *

Jack Barker was a Melba, Idaho, farm boy, the son of a Mormon farmer. Jack recalled his dad bragging that his own great-grandfather had ridden with the Prophet. There was no better Mormon pedigree. He also remembered the blow—a massive backhand slap—that had knocked the religion out of him. It had been during a public event at Temple Square in downtown Salt Lake City. He had been looking up at the golden statue that crowned the Tabernacle, the trumpet-blowing angel Moroni.

"Dad, do you think that when Moroni blows the golden horn on judgment day he'll blow pigeon shit all over the Hotel Utah across the street?" Jack pointed across the square when the vicious slap put him down on the sidewalk. Mouths gaping, his mother and sisters gasped audibly in surprise, but didn't speak.

"Get up," was all his father had said. "We don't joke about our faith—ever."

* * *

That day, fifteen years ago, Jack had vowed to leave the church, immediately after escaping the control of his father. Now, at age twenty-five, he didn't have many friends among the inmates, but then he didn't want to. Ray was different, a small man like himself, and not given to bragging or threatening. They thought themselves kindred souls and became best friends. Ray had once asked him about his nickname.

"They call me Scotty because I'm a piper."

"What does that mean? You can play the bagpipes or something? Cool, even if they sound like you're killing a pig."

"Not that kind of piper. When I got assigned to my cell, there was a guy on the same tier who decided he was going to own me. You probably know the type, lots of tattoos, big muscles and no brains. They come in all colors, but they are the sharks, and we're bait fish."

"The carnivores," Ray said. He also hated and feared such men.

"So this con, I'll call him Junior, decided I was going to be his bitch. Maybe that would have meant giving him blow jobs in the shower, or my commissary, maybe just my desserts or

55

smokes. Anyway, he was making my life uncomfortable every chance he got when there was no guard around. It got bad. That's how I met Fast Eddie. He saw what was happening, so he took me aside and explained what I needed to do."

"So what did you do?" Pinky leaned in. What was to come was for his ears only.

"I managed to get a piece of steel pipe from the machine shop. I watched and waited until Junior was taking an afternoon nap. Then I snuck into his cell and beat the living shit out of him. Everybody on the tier knew who did it—and why. But nobody bothers me now that I'm a piper."

"What did Junior say happened to him when the guards asked?"

"He did the right thing." Jack's tone conveyed a grudging admiration for Junior's adherence to an unwritten convict code. You didn't rat on another con. "He said he slipped and hit his head on the steel commode."

"And the guards believed him?"

"Don't know. Must have, because nothing was ever said after that, and Junior never tried any of that shit again."

* * *

Jack thought he knew how Ray got the nickname, 'Pinky.' They had been cellmates for some months now. In the close quarters of a two-man cell, privacy was minimal. Ray's lower body was a mass of pink scar tissue. The sides and tops of his legs, buttocks and groin were uniformly scarred. There were also the smaller mottled spots on his hands, arms, chest and back.

"Would you be willing to tell me about your scars?" Jack asked softly. Even though they shared a cell, all cons knew that some things were personal and boundaries needed to be respected. Ray didn't respond, seeming not to have heard, and Jack didn't ask again.

Days later, Ray answered the question. "When I was six, we lived in base housing at Fort Sill, Oklahoma, where my father was a drill instructor. He wasn't a patient man. I'd wet my bed. My mother tried not giving me anything to drink after dinner, but nothing worked, until I hit puberty and it just stopped.

"My father thought I could stop anytime if I'd wanted to, so it ticked him off. In the morning, Mom would try to get me cleaned up and hide the evidence before he got home from his morning run. This one morning he found me, wet again, before Mom did."

Pinky paused, staring up at the cell ceiling as if counting the tiles. Scotty waited patiently, imagining the pain that retelling the story must bring his cell mate.

"He went absolutely ape shit. He started screaming and I started crying. He dragged me to the bathroom, put me in the tub and turned the water on full blast. I guess he wanted to wash me off. All the time he's screaming at me about being lazy. The water was on full hot, 140 degrees. He was holding me down and I was screaming, 'No Daddy, I'm sorry Daddy!' and then, I was just screaming. My mom ran in and tried to draw him away from the tub. She was screaming, I was screaming, he was yelling; and some neighbor calls the MP's. When Dad smacked Mom, she started beating on him, and I was still screaming in the tub when the MP's arrived."

After a long pause, his tone changed to almost conversational, as he left that moment and came back to the present.

"My ass and the backs of my legs—where I was pressed tight to the porcelain—were protected from the scalding water, and I'm not scarred there, lucky for me. The small scars on my arms, back and chest are from water splashes. The MP's arrested Dad and took me to the base hospital. My mom finally left the rotten bastard after that, and we went to live with my grandparents in Spokane. My old man was sent to Leavenworth for what he did. Mom told me years later that he didn't do well inside."

"What happened to him?"

"He slipped."

* * *

"Where were we?" asked Eddie. The old con and his two students met as usual at Eddie's favorite picnic table in the prison yard. Eddie's back faced the prison; his students' backs were to the harbor. Scotty and Pinky knew by now that the harbor view represented the only freedom that Eddie enjoyed.

"We're up through rule six," Pinky said.

"I'm almost done, fellas: rule seven. All banks have cameras that you can't avoid. That's why I said to change your appearance for inside the bank, so you can change it back when you get outside. Wear gloves when you're inside the bank. Be polite. Open the door for people when you go in. The more people who give the police a wrong description the better. Any questions?"

Scotty and Pinky looked at each other and shook their heads.

"Last rule. Print your demand note in good size letters. Your note should be simple. Something like, 'This is a robbery. Keep smiling. No dye pack. If I get red, you get dead.' Show the teller the note, but you keep it. Give them a brown paper grocery bag for the money and tell them you're going to open it before you leave so they'll think twice about passing bait money with the dye pack. But you're really not going to do that. Just grab the bag and get the hell out of there."

* * *

"Fast Eddie's eight rules for success," intoned Scotty. "Eddie, how did you finally get caught?"

"The rules didn't fail me, if that's what you're wondering. My luck just ran out. I'm in San Francisco, and I just robbed the

58

First Interstate Bank. I've got my escape planned and the robbery went fine. I was in and out in two minutes—'Fast Eddie,' remember! I've got one block to walk to the bus stop and I'll be in the clear. Unbeknownst to me, there was a liquor store holdup going on up the street. The crook runs right over the top of me. We both dropped our bags and soon we're fighting over all this cash on the sidewalk. About that time, the police roll up. What are the odds of that?"

Eddie hung his head and the conversation paused. Then he eyeballed the silent pair. "Okay, what happened to you?"

Scotty spoke up first. "I got caught on my first job, The Bank of Idaho in Boise. I had to wait in line. When it was my turn, I go up to the window and there's this old bag of a teller. Glasses, iron gray hair, no smile. I passed her my note, and I was shaking while she reads it. Finally she looked up, stared at me with this hard look, and started shaking her head. I tapped the note with my fingers, like 'pay attention to this.' She looked me right in the eye and calls out, 'Next,' sweet as you please."

Scotty rubbed the back of his neck, clearly agitated at the memory. "She's not taking me seriously at all, like she's my third-grade teacher or and I just told her 'the dog ate my homework.' So I leaned over the counter and reach into her cash drawer and start grabbing the money myself. She slammed the cash drawer shut on my hand. I screamed and pulled out my busted hand and about $100 in bills. As I run out, I drop all but $40. When I got pinched a block away, I'm still holding my hand, crying like baby. It was a mess."

Eddie just smiled and looked out toward the harbor.

"I guess it's my turn," and Pinky raised his hands up and out and grinned in an advance apology for the fiasco he was about to admit. "I started in Spokane, my home town. Anyway, I was robbing this Washington Trust Bank. I passed my note and a brown paper bag. I was trying to keep one eye on the teller and another on the lobby. I looked away for just a second, and when I looked back at the teller, she passed me a brown bag and I run out. I got around the corner to my girlfriend's car and we got away. When I opened the bag, the teller had passed me her sack lunch. I got a banana, a baloney sandwich and a package of Ho-Ho's. Two days later my girlfriend gets popped in the car and gives me up so she can get off on a misdemeanor possession rap."

Eddie shakes his head and places a fatherly hand on the shoulder of each con. "What a pair you two are. But hey, it's not your fault" Eddie laughs. "You were probably not breast-fed, or you were toilet-trained too early. Maybe you didn't get a hot lunch in school."

"Exactly," replies Scotty. "We're just victims of social forces beyond our control!"

All three break into a laughter at the sound of their own bullshit.

* * *

Unlike Eddie, Scotty and Pinky had drawn only three-year sentences for unarmed bank robbery. They both expected to be paroled after two years. Their prospects for the future were a common topic after lights out each night.

"What's your plan, Pinky? Are you going to change tires at Les Schwab, work in a call center or flip burgers?" Scotty paused, to add drama to the moment. "Let me hear you practice saying, 'Would you like fries with that?'"

"Scotty, I'm going to rob another bank, that's what I'm going to do. I've been working on a plan. Hell, it's unique. I'll be floating down a river while the cops are checking bus stations and stolen car reports. I'll walk out of the bank and after two blocks I'm at the river. I get in my canoe, bait my hook and fish all the way downstream. I plan to put the money in a bag, throw it in the water and tow it behind me. If somehow I got stopped, I'd cut the line and the money would be gone. Pretty smart eh?"

His friend nodded, showing approval for the ingenuity of the plan. "I admire your honesty and the sheer genius of your plan."

"You want in? It's a two-man job. A fifty-fifty split and I already have the bank picked out. No girlfriends, though. Nobody ever knows about this but us."

"I'm in. I love the excitement of being a robber." Scotty leaning over from the cement shelf that served as a desk in the cell.

"Welcome aboard. When we're out we'll make a 'to do' list, but for now nothing goes on paper. We keep everything in our heads. You'll parole to Idaho, and I'll end up back in Spokane. The bank... it's in Priest River, Idaho."

"Priest River? What makes that little bank worth doing?"

"There's a big mill—Simpson Lumber—right across the river from town. Every two weeks the bank loads up on bills to cover the pay checks the millworkers will show up wanting to cash."

"You're going to be in a canoe, waiting for me under the bridge that runs from town to the mill. From the bank, I'm going to walk the one block to the river, lose my disguise and then we're going to float down the river to the Albeni Falls Dam. We'll carry the canoe around the dam and then you'll drive away. I'll float down to Newport. You've not been at the bank so you're not a suspect. At Newport, I'll load up the canoe and drive home."

"So I park my car at this dam. Then how do I get upriver to town in the canoe, paddle upstream?" Scotty asked.

"I'll drive you and the canoe past Priest River to this little town, Laclede. We'll put the canoe in the water there and you'll float down to town, fishing all the way. I'll have my fishing gear and extra clothes for after the job in the canoe. Once you're in the water, I'll drive down river to Newport, park and then ride my bike back to Priest River."

61

"I like it, Pinky. That puts the canoe and the cars in the right places without us showing our faces in town before the job. Brilliant!"

* * *

They both got released to Federal Parole supervision. Scotty went to Coeur d'Alene, Idaho, and Pinky went to Spokane. Scotty had applied himself while doing his time and come out a qualified denturist. A dental lab in Hayden, just above Coeur d'Alene, hired him straight away.

Pinky got a job swamping out a bar and restaurant in Spokane. Although this work involved his being around hard liquor, he had no history of alcohol or drug abuse, so the job was approved.

They waited until their paroles had terminated before making anything more than a token phone call to stay in touch. They would be, in all regards, model parolees who said and did exactly what the government wanted.

* * *

Five months later, the ringing of the phone interrupted his nap. Scotty blinked his eyes to clear the granules of sleep and picked up the receiver.

"It's Pinky. Are you ready for our joint venture? Sorry, I shouldn't say joint."

"I'm still up for it. Remind me why we're doing this, now that we're clean and free and don't have to?"

"Because we can and because we're smarter than they are. We like the thrill, and counting money is better than sex, that's why."

"What do I need to do?"

Pinky provided Scotty a list of things he needed to acquire. The list included fishing gear, a fishing license, a vehicle and a waterproof bag. Pinky's own list included a two-man canoe, a bicycle, a vehicle that could carry both canoe and bicycle, and his disguise.

"Are we still doing this on a Friday?"

"Yup, payday for the mill. I'll make our withdrawal at 2 p.m., two hours before the shift ends and the crowd hits the bank," Pinky answered. Scotty couldn't see his partner's smile but Pinky's enthusiasm did come across in his voice

"When?"

"April 24. It's before summer vacation, to cut down on the number of picnickers, campers, hikers and bikers."

"I'll check in April 17 from a pay phone. What else?"

"I think we're good. I'll get the canoe, a bike, my disguise and a change of clothes. You be sure to get the stuff on your list. We'll talk again later. All right, I'm off. Take care, Scotty."

* * *

On April 17, Scotty entered the phone booth in the parking lot of the Wolf's Lodge steak house along I-90. Pinky picked up on the first ring.

"Are you at a pay phone?" Ever cautious, Scotty pressed his mouth to the phone in a conspiratorial gesture, as if he might be under surveillance by the thought police.

"Absolutely. That's road noise in the background."

"How are you doing on your supplies?"

"I've got everything on my list. How about you?"

"I've got a canoe that fits in the bed of my truck along with the bike. I've already got a seven-day fishing license: keeping it legal, after all." The smile on Pinky's face crept into his voice.

"I think we're set. I'll have a change of clothes in the canoe. I'll already be in part of my disguise. The rest will be in a roll I'll have on the bike. I'll be looking for you at the parking lot at 11 o'clock. We drive to Laclede and you push off by 12:30. The float should only take an hour, tops. There's no down-side to your being under the bridge early, but it would be a big problem if you're late."

"I'm allowing 90 minutes for my bike ride back to Priest River. I'll chain the bike up, so it looks like it belongs to a local. Then find a place to put on my disguise and hit the bank at 2 p.m. I'm in and out in three minutes or less, walk the one block down to the river and we're off."

"Let's go rob a bank."

"Just for shits and grins right?"

"Yup, more fun than a barrel of monkeys, carving teeth or mopping floors. See you next Friday."

* * *

April 24, Pinky leaned on the hood of his truck as he watched the river. He'd turned around twice to the sounds of vehicles pulling off the highway and into the parking lot, but still no sign of Scotty. The hands on his watch marked the time as 11:15 a.m.

Just east of Laclede, Scotty stared across the hood of his truck at the flagman holding a sign that was still turned to the 'STOP' side. Having checked the map, he knew he'd need at least twenty minutes to make it to the dam. The map didn't show any way to bypass the road construction blockage. Research hadn't helped. Swearing hadn't worked. Prayer would probably be next.

Pinky's watch now showed 11:45. Scotty's truck was moving too fast for the turn into the lot. The squeal of the tires was lost in the blasts of the horn. Scotty parked alongside Pinky's truck and moved quickly into the passenger seat of the Dodge. Pressed for time, Pinky was already backing out before either man spoke.

"Sorry Pinky. There was road construction and a flagman. Do we still have time?"

"Barely, if the road back to Laclede is clear."

"It's clear."

"Then we should be okay. But if I can't make the schedule, I'm not going to force it. You're still under the bridge fishing. If something happens on my end, I'll just ride down to the river, signal you, and ride back to your truck.

"I'm good with that. Shit happens, right?"

A flagman was controlling traffic up ahead as they pulled off the highway at Laclede, crossed the tracks and stopped at the boat launch. Scotty was relieved to see the ramp and parking area empty. His relief was short lived. He remembered what he'd forgotten, and his head dropped to his chest.

"Pinky, do you remember the Laurel and Hardy movies? Remember how when Laurel would make a mistake, Hardy would roll his eyes and give his line, 'this is another fine mess you've gotten us into'?"

Pinky turned off the engine.

"Then Laurel gets tears in his eyes and sort of whimpers, 'I'm sorry Ollie. I didn't mean it.' Pinky, I forgot to get the fishing gear and the waterproof bag out of my truck back at the dam."

Pinky stared across the bench seat of the truck at Scotty, who now broke into faux tears.

"I'm sorry, Pinky. I didn't mean it."

"Well Scotty, all I can say is... this is another fine mess you've gotten us into." Pinky shook his head and smiled. "In two weeks, we'll try again, agreed?"

"Agreed."

"Come on, I'll buy you coffee in Newport. Then I'll show you the back road on the south side of the river so you can skip the road construction."

* * *

On Friday, May 8, Scotty pulled into the parking lot right on time. Loaded up, they headed for the boat ramp. It was noon when the canoe went into the water. Scotty had more than two hours to float the distance and get tied up in the shade under the bridge in Priest River.

"See you at two, Scotty."

"Just don't fall off the bike."

Scotty thought he'd learned the basics of paddling and how to keep the canoe pointed downstream. With the sun on his face he smiled and said to no one, "Hey, how hard can it be? I've got this."

The ski boat with its trailing skier came up on his rear. The driver of the boat waved when he roared past the canoe. Scotty returned the greeting and blissfully watched the passing boat and skier. He saw the boat's wake, but he had no clue about its power or the need to turn the canoe into the approaching wake.

The wake hit the canoe full on the side, rolling it over and dumping Scotty and the gear into the river. Cold water smacked him in the face as he went under. The fishing poles and tackle box sank immediately. The waterproof bag, paddle and clothes floated away. Scotty broke the surface, gasping for breath and shaking his head to clear his vision. The upside-down canoe momentarily provided a welcome platform for his arms while he tried to catch his breath.

"Son-of-a-bitch!" He spit the words out with a mouthful of water.

Jamie, the driver of the ski boat, saw the canoe overturn as he watched his buddy Andy skiing. "Oh man," Jamie exclaimed over the roar of the outboard motor and he cut the power. Jamie pointed back over the skier's shoulder. Andy looked, but didn't realize yet that the canoe was now gone from view. When Andy was in the boat, they headed back to the capsized canoe.

"Mister, are you alright?" Andy shouted as the boat came parallel to the canoe. "We didn't mean to sink you. Jeez, I'm sure sorry. We figured that you'd turn right into our wake. Oh, man."

Scotty didn't respond until Jamie brought the boat alongside the canoe. The boys grabbed the floating bow and stern, then working together, they righted the aluminum hull.

"Thanks for coming back, guys. I've never been in a canoe before," Scotty blew water from his nose and shook his head to clear his eyes. "Can you look for any clothes, or see if a green canvas bag is still floating around out there? I really don't want to lose my stuff."

"Yeah sure," Jamie called, and began to search the surface for any sign of the lost goods. "Andy, I see some stuff floating about ten yards downstream. Keep the boat alongside and I'll go grab what I can." From the bow of the ski boat he dove into the water.

"Can you get yourself back into the canoe while I'm holding it steady?" Andy asked.

"We'll find out." Scotty pulled himself out of the water. Flopping into the canoe, Scotty began check its contents to see what had been lost. In short order he had his answer...everything. His heart sank at the thought that once again he had managed to screw up Pinky's plan.

"I got some of the stuff," Jamie called as he side-stroked back to the canoe, trailing the green waterproof bag. "Is this yours?"

"Yeah good job. Did you see my clothes?"

"Just this, sorry, man. What else did you lose?" Catching his breath, he rested while holding onto the canoe.

"Two poles, tackle box, tennis shoes and a paddle."

"Jamie, there's the paddle! It's hung up on that dead tree about five yards back." Andy pointed to a spot upstream. With that, Jamie pushed off from the canoe and soon recovered the only paddle.

"Can you check down on the bottom?" Scotty called to the swimmer. Passing the paddle back to Scotty, Jamie disappeared under the water. Finally he broke the surface, shaking his head and blowing out his nose to clear the water. He handed up into the canoe a single pole and canvas shoes tied together by their laces.

"That's all I could find." He swam back to the rear of the ski boat.

Suddenly, a new worry invaded Scotty's mind. He checked his Timex and it was 1:25. His heart sank. Could he still make the rendezvous on time?

"How far is it to Priest River?"

"About four miles," was the reply.

"I'm worn out from my swim, fellas. Can you tow me into town behind your boat? I'll be fine with loading up my canoe, if I can just get a little rest going into town." Their response was immediate. Both young men were eager to atone for swamping the canoe.

"Sure, you sit in the front of your canoe and hold the ski rope. Jamie will drive slowly, and all you need to do is let go of the rope whenever you want."

"That's great, and we'll call it good on the lost fishing gear. Accidents happen, right?" For the first time since the accident, Scotty smiled.

Andy passed the handle of the towrope over as Jamie fired up the outboard motor. Scotty gingerly moved to the bow of the canoe while Andy stayed in the back of the boat and flashed a 'thumbs up' sign to Jamie. The rope pulled hard on Scotty's shoulders. He bent his back and positioned his knees to keep himself upright under the pull of the boat. They covered the four miles into Priest River in 20 minutes.

The bridge came into sight around a bend in the river. Scotty saw a boat launch and parking lot upstream from his actual destination. Letting go of the towrope, he pointed to the parking lot, raised his arm in a parting wave to the boys and slowly paddled for shore. When the boys were out of sight he started steering parallel to the shore until he reached the shadow of the bridge and tied up under the wide cement deck. He'd made it.

* * *

After leaving Laclede, Pinky drove through Priest River, Idaho and on past the dam. He'd traveled a total of 18 miles when he parked in the Safeway grocery lot in Newport, Washington. He checked that his disguise was securely bungee-corded to the handlebars of his bike. A length of chain and a keyed padlock had been wound around and secured to the seat post. In his cut-off jeans, T-shirt, baseball cap and sunglasses, he looked the part of a touring cyclist.

At 12:30, Pinky began riding from Newport back to Priest River, keeping to the outside of the fog line on the eastbound lane of the highway. He turned off at the east end of town where reeds and marsh slowed the flow of the Priest River as it joined the Pend Oreille River that flowed through town. Two blocks off the highway was a small strip mall. He chose the end of this single row of shops that tailed off from the parking lot down to the reeds and marsh where the two rivers merged.

It was 1:30 when Pinky chained his bike to a gas meter on the side of the building. He walked off into the privacy of the reeds and put his disguise on over what would be his fishing clothes. He kept his thin leather cycling gloves on and added a red-checkered flannel shirt, then tucked the shirttails into faded denim jeans. A quick getaway being essential, he had patiently opened the side seams of the jeans and glued in Velcro closure strips. After the robbery his shoes would be replaced by slipping on canvas shoes that were already in the canoe.

Walking to the edge of the reeds, he checked again for observers. With no one in sight, he put his cap back on and stepped onto the covered walk of the faux Western facade of

69

the strip mall. His watch showed 1:50 and the bank was a three-block walk west through the small downtown area. Under his arm, neatly folded, was a brown paper grocery bag. His demand note was printed in block letters on the side of the bag.

THIS IS A ROBBERY
MY GUN IS LOADED
NO DYE PACK OR YOU DIE
PUT MONEY IN THIS BAG

Pinky passed in front of the city hall and police station. At the corner were the two open bays of the fire department. When he turned left at the corner, the bank was now in view, a block down the street and half way to the bridge. Cutting diagonally across the intersection, Pinky continued down the block and turned to enter the bank's glass front door. He held the door open for a large woman in jeans and a Western-cut blouse who was leaving the bank. Then he put on his sunglasses.

"Thank you," she said.

"You're welcome," he replied with a smile, then stepped inside.

The small lobby held no customers. A single teller, ten steps ahead on his left, had her back to the lobby as she finished with a customer at the drive-through window. She was wearing the female equivalent of a leisure suit. Its canary-yellow polyester seemed to audibly clash with her mercurochrome orange hair. Across from the tellers, two desks filled the right side of the room. At the desk nearest the door, a middle-aged woman was talking on the phone. The second desk was vacant. Pinky stood at the teller window, waiting.

The teller half turned and acknowledged him. "I'll be right there."

He smiled and nodded in response. The grocery bag was unfolded from under his arm, note side up. In less than a minute, the drive-through transaction was completed.

"Now, how can I help you?" asked the overweight woman.

Pinky smiled and raised the top of the bag from the counter surface to put the demand note in the center of her field of view. He slid the bag across the counter, concealing his left hand below the counter. Cocking his right thumb and index finger, he mouthed, 'gun' and used the gesture to point toward his concealed left hand.

The color in her face faded. She stared at the note, and then looked up at Pinky. When she hesitated, he mouthed, 'now,' and she began filling the bag. He turned around and saw that the woman at the desk was still on the phone, her eyes fixed on the desk top. In a second, his eyes returned to the orange-haired teller who seemed to be moving in slow motion. When he spoke for the first time, his voice was soft and low.

"All of it. The envelopes of big bills, too." He made the gun gesture again.

When she passed the bag, her unblinking eyes rolled back in her head and she crumpled loudly to the floor. Pinky leaned over the counter to see if this was a ruse, and she had really dived for cover after hitting a silent alarm. It was not.

"Oh my God, she's had a heart attack," yelled Pinky, his volume amplified by the bank's small interior. "I'll run to the fire department for help!"

Bag in hand, he ran towards the exit, almost colliding with the woman at the desk who had dropped the phone and come around her desk heading for the teller cages.

"Thank you, thank you! Yes please, get help!"

Out on the sidewalk, the bridge was a single block downhill to his right. Instead, he turned left and ran up the hill to the fire station. An ambulance was getting a wash outside on the street.

"Help, the bank teller had a heart attack. We need an EMT!" Then Pinky turned and ran back toward the bank, as if leading rescuers. Checking quickly for any audience and seeing none, he continued to the river and walked down the slope of the bank to the water.

Halfway down the bank he got his first view of Scotty and the canoe. Grabbing the Velcro seams of his jeans, he stripped to his cut-offs, throwing the pants into the canoe followed by the long-sleeved shirt, gloves and shoes. He handed the grocery bag to Scotty. With one foot in the water he untied the bow of the canoe from the small willow tree that held it, pushed off from the bank and climbed into the canoe.

The firm push served to turn them gently into the current. Pinky loaded his disguise into the waterproof bag where Scotty had already placed the bag of money.

"How did we do, Pinky?"

"Jeez, I didn't get the chance to look. You tell me."

Scotty glanced quickly into the money bag. "I see lots of hundreds, but that's all I can tell right now. We've got to go." Sealing the bag, Scotty eased it out of sight into the green of the river.

"Everything's wet. What happened?"

"I went for an unplanned swim," Scotty smiled. "We lost some clothes and fishing gear. How'd you do?"

"It went as smooth as baby Jesus in velvet pants. There was one small wild card, but it actually played to our advantage."

"Tell me."

In response, Pinky narrated the incident with the teller.

"So you went for help? Why?"

"I guess because I was there. It needed doing and I still have to live with whatever I did or didn't do."

"You'll probably get extra ice cream in heaven, or at least one day a year out of hell for that one good deed."

At the dam, Pinky guided the canoe to the boat launch. The waterproof bag was hoisted back inside and together they lifted the canoe up and out of the water. At the parking lot they stopped, transferring the waterproof bag and the one remaining fishing rod into the cab of Scotty's truck. Then they carried the canoe along a descending path and put back in the water below the dam.

As Scotty turned to walk back to his truck, Pinky spoke. "Like we planned, we'll launder the money at Cactus Pete's in Jackpot." Scotty had always liked this part of the plan. He'd never been to Nevada or inside a real casino.

"See you there one week from tomorrow. I'll have the money counted and split into equal shares."

Pinky smiled. "You'll be the guy in the coffee shop, wearing the shit-eating grin, right?" Having trusted Scotty for protection in prison, trusting him now with their money was not an issue for him.

"Pinky, seriously now, what if we gamble and lose?"

"Scotty, if either of us had wanted to really make crime pay, we'd have gone to law school. We're in this for the fun, anyway. Well, I guess it's time for me to float on down the river."

"That's better than going up the river, right?"

"Absolutely, I'll see you in Jackpot." Pushing off, Pinky hopped into the canoe.

"Pinky, do you think Eddie would be proud of us?" shouted Scotty.

"I think he would. When he gets out, we'll have a good story to share. Happy trails, pilgrim," Pinky called over his shoulder as his paddle bit into the green of the Pend Oreille River.

"Oh, and Scotty, don't forget to ask me about this little bank in Riggins, Idaho. It's right on the Salmon River. I hear it's beautiful there in the late spring. We really should do this again."

The End

Author's Notes

Pinky and the Piper puts together a number of true bank robbery events. The failed robberies that Eddie, Scotty and Pinky describe are true cases from my days in San Francisco. I was the Army CID agent that responded to and investigated the child scalding case. The North Idaho and Terminal Island Prison settings are places I have visited or worked.

6. Idaho Catch and Release

Edna Kirkland loved the modest stucco bungalow she and her late husband Duane had bought 60 years ago with his GI bill benefits. The modest two-bedroom house on a quiet street in Rexburg, Idaho, held good memories that she wrapped around herself like a shawl.

The postman delivered her Reader's Digest magazines and their condensed books. A neighbor boy cut the grass. Ladies from the Relief Society helped her with grocery shopping and drove her to church on Sundays. Life was good. The sure knowledge that someday her future held a joyous reunion with Duane and the Heavenly Father was all she needed.

The regular postman was gone today. A young substitute delivery person, in postal blue-gray, opened the door to her mailbox on the gatepost. In went today's copy of the Deseret News, a circular from the local market and a legal-size manila envelope.

The noon sun was shining as Edna removed the mail from the box. Comfortable in a housedress, she sat down in one of the two metal chairs that bracketed her front door. Edna's calico cat lay in the sun on the corner of the porch.

On top of the stack was the circular from the market. Jell-O, white bread and fruit cocktail were on special again. Milk at 99 cents a gallon was the market's loss leader. She usually read the Deseret News next, but not today. The mysterious manila envelope in her lap beckoned. Its address side down, Edna took her time unsealing the glued flap.

"If I'm careful, I can reuse this," she said to the cat. The cat ignored Edna in favor of licking its paws

The first thing she saw as the contents slipped from inside the envelope was a Christmas card.

"Now that's strange, it's not Christmas for three more months." The cat opened one eye at the sound of Edna's voice.

"Merry Christmas," was printed in large black letters on glossy white card stock. Opening the card, Edna thought she needed to adjust her bifocals. Inside the card, stretching from edge to edge, was the image of a huge erect penis, starting at its tip and ending at a torso. At the centerfold of the card, a large red bow was tied around the member. Below the image, in the same bold black print were the words, "You big prick!"

"Oh my." Edna covered her mouth and swallowed hard. She hadn't seen anything like that for years.

The circular, newspaper and a half dozen 8-by-10 glossy photos from the mysterious envelope all tumbled from her lap and onto the cat as Edna passed out. The cat looked back toward the source of the attack with a mixture of disgust and puzzlement as she ran from the porch.

* * *

A Rexburg police officer picked up the offensive material. Because the envelope was addressed to her next-door neighbor, Edna was excluded as a suspect. Two days later, the neighbor was confronted with the envelope by the U.S. postal inspector at the city police station. There was no return address on the envelope. A Lake City, Idaho, postmark was the only indication of the envelope's origin. Sweating in the police station, the neighbor denied any knowledge of the pornography.

Postal Inspector Duane Finch needed to get the man talking, so he started with an opener from, "Interviewing 101."

Standard technique No. 1: "Pretend to want the subject's help. Ask how he/she thinks the crime or evidence can be explained."

"The envelope was addressed to you and sent to your home. How do you suppose that happened?"

"I have no idea," the sweating man responded as he drummed his fingertips on the table.

Standard technique No. 2: "Help the subject rationalize their behavior." He picked up one of the six pictures showing the young woman and her male partner.

"Just between you and me, how can she do that? Haven't you ever been just a little curious yourself?"

"Never." His chin jutted forward in indignation and his voice grew louder. "Those images are vile and an offense before God. I'm a family man, an elder in the church and a supervisor with the Bureau of Reclamation."

Standard technique No. 3: "Minimize the seriousness of the offense."

"Come on, Brother Morris, help me out here. You didn't produce the photos and that's who the government wants. We just need your help to find the real bad guys. We're not interested in you."

Inspector Finch was lying, but he didn't care. This was a "permissible deception" allowed by the law. He found the pictures disgusting, vile even. Those who partook of such filth were as guilty as the producers.

Intentionally prolonging his silence, Finch watched and waited for some telltale signal that Morris was ready to talk. The signal came when Morris hung his head, sighed and all of his facial muscles relaxed into a mask of resignation.

Finch pounced. "You'll feel better when this is over. Why don't you tell me about the pictures?"

A flood of tears and answers came out. Gilbert Morris had given up.

"The pictures come every 90 days. They are always of the same blonde female and the same male partner. I responded to a pop-up ad on a porn site. I pay by postal money order, $100 per envelope. The payee's name is always left blank, as instructed. I send the money to a mailbox in Lake City."

His head in his hands, his voice was now a soft monotone, devoid of inflection, between sobs. Finch had seen suspects overcome by shame before. Morris's chin dropped to his chest, trembling, and he pressed his palms flat to the table top.

"You did the right thing," Finch had learned how to sound sympathetic. A few kind words delivered in a soothing tone and an understanding nod would help Morris be a willing witness at any coming trial. He left Morris slumped over and crying.

Finch passed the local detective outside the interview room door. "Let the shit-bag go home after he stops crying."

* * *

"The Assistant United States Attorney in Boise, upon reviewing the case, kicked it up to his boss. The U.S. Attorney, like his assistant and until recently their Chief Federal Judge, were all church elders. The AUSA knew crimes of moral turpitude were of special interest to his boss. Sin was, after all, the taproot of crime. The pending case against a North Idaho sheriff who tolerated gambling and brothels in his county was just another sign of the sickness that resided among the gentiles of Idaho's panhandle.

"What's the robbing of a bank compared to the robbing of righteousness that destroys a family; now that's crime!" The U.S. Attorney spoke with a sweeping arm gesture and finished by slamming his fist into the tabletop.

The boss's words, delivered over caffeine-free Pepsi, still rang in his ears. The AUSA was confident Morris, having shamed the faith as well as himself and his family, would be indicted. And he was right.

* * *

Two years ago, it had been a busy Wednesday for Christie Craig. She left the ski shop she and her husband operated and took packages and catalog mailings to the post office. She dropped off Bruno, their German Shepherd, at the vet to have his teeth cleaned and his nails trimmed.

The errands had to fit into her day. This was a busy time of year. The snow was good and the ski hill was crowded. Christie knew her work day would end well after dark. She hoped she and Wiley's long-planned special evening, a visit to the Water's Edge Restaurant in downtown Lake City, could still take place.

* * *

There had been a rash of car break-ins and acts of vandalism at the city parking lot that separated the boat launch ramps from the Water's Edge Resort's parking lot. Patrolman Archie Amundson found himself surveilling the lot from an unheated shed. Archie checked the improvised peephole that faced the restaurant's parking. The dining room's floor-to-ceiling windows were now solid silver mirrors of glowing condensation. He could no more see in than diners could see out. Four feet outside the glass a low split-rail fence kept cars back from the windows. Archie's parka, pack boots, gloves and fur cap were his only protection from the ten-degree chill of night. He heard the parking lot ice crunch as a Land Rover came down Bridge Street, pulled up to the rail and parked outside the frosted dining room windows.

"Another lucky couple of skiers dining out after a day on the slopes," he muttered. Watching the driver and passenger doors open and the young couple exit, he wished he was one of them.

They were both naked except for pack boots, gloves and red ski caps. Bending over, she placed her hands on the fence rail and, widening her stance, began to wave her butt slowly back and forth. Her partner joined the fun by mounting her from behind with visible joy. Off came his gloves as his hands moved to cup her breasts.

79

"They're having sex - and they're good at it." Officer Amundson opened the shed door. "Stop! Police!" he shouted.

Fifty yards of smooth ice-covered parking lot separated the shed from the lovers.

They turned their heads. With a mighty shove, the man propelled his accomplice over the rail. She somersaulted to a landing at the base of the dining-room window. Her cowardly lover ran to the Land Rover.

Archie slipped and slid across the lot. The Land Rover backed up and began to drive away. Scrambling to her feet, the snow-dusted woman hopped the rail and began chasing her partner's car, which headed out of the parking lot. She caught the Rover, climbed in and they drove away, disappearing into the night. Unfortunately she and the distinctive bumper sticker stuck in Amundson's memory years later. "I love my German Shepherd" was the implied meaning of the words, red heart image and dog silhouette.

* * *

Wiley Craig loved being an amateur photographer. He was an amateur only in the sense his photo play with Christie and her four-legged lover, Bruno, would never be seen by a wider audience. The money from the pornography business kept their lifestyle afloat. It was expensive to have a house on the lake, imported cars and a condo on the mountain at the Ski Village.

"It's too bad that someone's private sexual conduct can be illegal," he said to his lover over the viewfinder.

"Thank God it is illegal, baby, or we wouldn't make any money from our family pictures." She was bent over a brown leather hassock, head down and butt up. Bruno vigorously pursued the task at hand.

"Just a couple of more shots and we'll call it a night. Slide your butt up a little higher if you can." The image he wanted appeared in the viewfinder of his 35 mm camera.

Wiley had purchased a high-resolution printer that allowed him to print images on pre-cut card stock or photographic paper. He was sure the investment would pay off.

Their customer base expanded, so the Craigs could now draw from an existing inventory of images. These went to the new club members. Long-standing customers clamored for new, more perverse offerings. But there were only so many positions and combinations that bodies were capable of taking.

"Beautiful, a perfect money shot, my darling! Good boy Bruno!" Christie had contributed the business name, "Puppy Love," and the original idea. Bruno's predecessor, a beagle named Sparky, had inspired her. Sparky faithfully followed her around the house, even standing guard as Christie soaked in their claw-footed tub. When she stepped out of the tub one afternoon, Sparky began to hump her leg. Christie was never one to miss an opportunity; Puppy Love was born.

* * *

After sending Bruno to his dog bed for the night, the couple shared a glass of wine. The view through their picture windows was out over the lake. Moonlight playing across the water and onto snow-covered hills was a million-dollar still-life image painted in silvers and greys.

Christie's hair was still damp from her post-session shower. She sat with legs curled under her in one of the two leather armchairs that flanked the big stone fireplace.

"Have you gotten any orders from the Christmas card sample that you enclosed with the last delivery?"

"So far only three bites, but it's early yet and our fans just got the packet a month ago. I think it will do even better than the birthday card we put out last year. A birthday cake never looked better, my dear." Wiley raised his glass in a toast. The card had shown a smiling Christie in a yoga pose with a large red candle protruding from the cheeks of her firm butt. Above the image the card read, "Happy Birthday, Enjoy your Cake!"

* * *

Postal Inspector Finch sent a Request for Assistance (RFA), to his counterparts in Spokane, the nearest field office to Lake City, Idaho. Inspector Bob Vasquez was assigned to answer the RFA. The request opened with a brief overview of the case. Next came the specifics of the request.

"Please attempt to identify, locate and interview the holder of Box 451 at 'The Mail Box,' 112 Superior St., Lake City, Idaho. Conduct local records checks with city, county and state law enforcement concerning the box holder(s). Please attempt to identify the adult female shown in the enclosed image, marked as evidence Exhibit 9. Based on the success of your inquiries, please coordinate any future investigative efforts with the undersigned. Your response is requested to be received by December 15, 1989."

Lake City is about 50 miles from Spokane. Inspector Vasquez already had an interview scheduled in Downey, Idaho, a suburb of Lake City, for later in the week. He'd handle the RFA during the same trip.

The Mail Box was a private business. You rented a box and paid in cash. Your identification was not checked against your box rental slip. You could pick up mail 24/7 from the small lobby. You were buying privacy.

Box 451 had been rented continuously for the past two years by Mr. Robert Dawg, 220 First St., Priest River, Idaho. Vasquez already knew the address. It was the city of Priest River Police Station and City Hall.

"So have you ever seen Mr. Dawg?" Vasquez asked the store clerk.

"I've only worked here for six months and I've never seen him. I'm always in the back, except when somebody rings the service bell to rent a box."

Vasquez thanked the clerk for her time and moved on to the Lake City Police.

Vasquez was familiar to Valerie, the department's records clerk/receptionist. She waved him through and he walked down the hall toward the office of Chief of Police Bill Price. Vasquez, the chief and Sergeant Amundson were old friends. They'd all started their careers in law enforcement as California Highway Patrol officers.

"Hello Bill."

"Hey Bob, good to see you," Price got up from his desk to shake hands. "What can we do for you?"

Vasquez recapped the RFA and what he had learned at The Mail Box. Showing the photo from the RFA to Price got Vasquez only a vague sign of recognition.

"She could be a lot of people. We don't really know if the material is being produced locally or just mailed from here. Archie is in the coffee room. Let's see if he has any ideas."

Archie Amundson thought she looked familiar. He lowered his head, concentrating hard to match the face to a memory. "Wait a minute. I've got it now. That's the girl from the Water's Edge parking lot!"

He described his cold nights staked out at the city lot by the Water's Edge Resort and the two naked lovers.

"This was two years ago. They had a white Land Rover with one of those "I love my dog" bumper stickers. Hers had a silhouette of a German Shepherd. I couldn't make out the plate, except that it was a '7-B' county number, so the rig was local. I never followed up, but I always thought that it could have been the Craigs. They run a ski shop in the town and have a house on the lake. I'm sure that's her in the pictures. Christie Ann Craig is her name." Amundson and Price both agreed that the woman in the evidence photo and Christie Ann Craig were one and the same.

Before leaving the station, Vasquez determined the Craigs had no local criminal records, paid their taxes and were active in the chamber of commerce. By all indications they were hard-working young marrieds who were doing well with a retail ski shop and catalog business. He also obtained color driver's license photos of them and confirmed their ownership of a 1990 Land Rover and a 1987 Porsche.

Next, Vasquez showed the license picture of Christie Craig to the local postmaster. Christie was a regular. She dropped off boxes and manila envelopes, at least weekly. And yes, she was a dog owner. Things were speeding up.

Vasquez walked the two blocks from the post office to the ski shop. Legally he couldn't question the Craigs about the case without advising them of their Miranda rights. But he could get a visual on Mrs. Craig and perhaps the dog. The parka that Vasquez wore on this cold November day allowed him to pass as a ski shop browser. Christie was behind the counter and Bruno was asleep in a corner of the shop. The agent recognized them from the evidence photo.

He walked back toward the police station on a route to pass behind the ski shop. There was the Land Rover with the "I love my dog" bumper sticker. The silhouette on the sticker pictured a German Shepard.

Stopping at the county assessor's office, Vasquez obtained addresses and legal descriptions on three properties the couple owned. This identifying information would be needed by the U.S. Attorney's Office for subpoenas and warrants. He'd confer with Inspector Finch in Salt Lake before going further.

"I found your perps, and we are ready to move ahead with search warrants. Here's what I've got," Vasquez related by phone the next morning. "What do you think?"

"Good job, Bob. With the affidavit you'll prepare and based on my dealing with the U.S. Attorney's Office in Idaho, I think we're good to go. I'll write up the warrant request for searches at the three properties and for any bank accounts we can locate. I'll also ask for arrest warrants. Once I've got the warrants in hand, I'll let you know. Can you arrange raid teams from your office and get help from the locals?"

"No problem."

Duane Finch presented the information he had to the U.S. Attorney's Office in Pocatello, Idaho. It was all there, and probable cause was clearly established. AUSA Mark Callister's only concern was not knowing if these two apparent pillars of the community had been stupid enough to leave any evidence lying around. Still, he took the matter to a federal grand jury. Based on the evidence Inspector Finch presented, an indictment was returned.

Wiley and Christie were each named in all counts of a 7-count indictment. Each count alleged violations of 18 USC 1465 and 1466; Production and Transportation of Obscene Matter for Sale or Distribution. One count for each item that had dropped from Edna Kirkland's hands in Rexburg.

Inspector Vasquez coordinated a raid team: two city detectives, three sheriff's deputies, two deputy U.S Marshals, two animal control specialists and four other postal inspectors besides himself. Vasquez agreed to take the lead in assigning duties. The 14 law-enforcement individuals had their designated tasks. He'd initiate the raid early on a Sunday morning, the better to get both Craigs and their two vehicles all together in one place.

* * *

The authorities arrived in four cars. They parked at the entrance to the driveway out of sight of the house. A light snow, new, white and silent, was falling. One of the sheriff's deputies had positioned himself outside the lake house's wide garage doors. Another deputy was at the back door of the home. Two city police detectives, one in front and one at the rear were outside the ski shop. Another sheriff's deputy and a deputy U.S. Marshal waited outside the Craigs' ski chalet.

* * *

Wiley Craig knew the moment he opened his front door that he'd need a good criminal attorney. Seven crew-cuts and one petite woman with a ponytail, in identical dark blue raid jackets, waited at the door. Not until the raiders were inside would Wiley be able to tell by the bold yellow lettering on the back of each jacket who were local police and who were feds. The two men at the back were there for Bruno.

"Mr. Craig, I'm U.S. Postal Inspector Robert Vasquez." He held up his open badge case to show Wiley a photo identification and gold badge.

Standing in the open front door in his robe, pajamas and slippers, Wiley Craig stayed silent.

Vasquez remained professional, all the while thinking, "You sick son-of-a-bitch."

"We are here to serve search and arrest warrants on you and your wife." Putting his credentials away, Vasquez produced the warrants from inside his jacket, handing copies of the folded documents to Craig

The other seven agents entered the foyer. As Wiley Craig looked over the warrants, Vasquez spoke into the small microphone positioned on the inside of his wrist.

"Raid teams, this is Vasquez ...go."

"Heard"—"Roger that," sounded in his earpiece as the other raid teams simultaneously executed search warrants at the Craigs' business and mountain top ski chalet.

"Please call your wife and ask her to come down." Vasquez motioned the female agent to move forward.

With the warrants now in the suspect's hands, Vasquez quickly moved through the foyer and into the house. Two of the agents proceeded to let their cohorts at the garage doors and back door into the house. The search commenced.

"Is there anyone else in the house now besides your wife?"

Wiley Craig shook his head. "Christie, we have company. The feds are here. They want you to come down." His voice was deliberately louder than normal. If Christie had to face the feds, he wanted her to do it decently covered and not by surprise in their bedroom.

Trudy, the female agent, made her way up a flight of stairs to the landing outside the couple's open-loft bedroom. The half-wall of the loft, visible from the main floor, provided privacy without enclosing any of the rough-hewn exposed-beam ceilings.

Two animal control specialists crouched, out of view, on the stairs behind the female inspector. Each animal control officer wore a protective bite-sleeve over one forearm and had a leash or a muzzle in his back pocket. The lead man clutched a four-foot long catchpole with a plastic-coated wire noose protruding from its end. The second agent held a drawn pistol in his free hand, just in case it became necessary to see if Bruno could really eat bullets.

Christie Craig stood up from the edge of the couple's king-size bed and stepped into her slippers. What she was wearing under her gold velour robe was not visible to the agent when she topped the stairs and looked into the loft bedroom.

Bruno slept in the corner of the bedroom. The big Shepherd, roused by the visitors, moved to the bedside. He stood silently by Christie, watching the strange woman on the landing, ears back, his chest rumbling with a low growl.

"Mrs. Craig, you need to come with me, please," the female agent directed.

"Don't say anything, darling," came her husband's voice from down below. Christie swung her eyes briefly to the agent, her glance conveying indifference or maybe boredom. She stood and rested her right hand on Bruno's wide shoulders, staring at the intruding agent.

"If you don't mind, I'd like to pee and then get dressed," and she began walking across the loft toward the walk-in closet, dressing area and bathroom. Bruno followed, attentive for directions from Christie

As she stepped out of the loft and into the side gallery, her robe fell to the floor. Christie Craig stood naked before the female inspector. "Will that be all right, or would you like to watch me pee? I will if you like."

The agent gave no response save a small sigh. "Bill, what do you want me to do?" she called over to Inspector Vasquez on the floor below.

"Trudy, she can use the bathroom and get dressed, as long as you check the bath, drawers and closet for weapons before you give her access."

Then Vasquez continued: "Mrs. Craig, we'll let you use the toilet and dress if you cooperate by staying where you are until Inspector Bullock checks the bathroom. Then you can close the door and do whatever you need. When you come out, point to the drawers or closet that you need, but don't open anything until Inspector Bullock tells you that you can go ahead. Do you understand what I need you to do?"

"Yes Daddy, I understand. I'll be good—I promise." She managed to combine boredom and sexuality in one tone.

"Okay, Trudy, you can let her go."

Bruno's eyes followed Trudy, and the rumble in his chest grew as the agent walked past Christie to check the bathroom for weapons. When the bathroom had been checked, Bruno followed his mistress. As the door shut, the dog turned and sat down in front of it, his eyes never leaving the intruder.

Trudy held her position in the dressing room area, just outside the bathroom, She surveyed the contents of two of the four closets until a firm but gentle pressure filled her crotch. Bruno was inhaling deeply and when she jumped, startled by the contact, the big Shepherd stared fixedly and began to pant. Love was in the air. Returning the dog's stare, she moved her hand to the butt of her pistol, just in case.

While Christie Craig was dressing, Wiley had been allowed to call his attorney. Not surprisingly, the attorney instructed Wiley that absolutely nothing be said to anyone, outside his presence.

"Wiley, ask the agent where they are taking you."

"They're talking us to their office across from you."

"Fourth and Lakeside?"

"Exactly"

"I'll be waiting for you—and remember, not a word. We'll talk then."

"Right."

* * *

Under supervision, both the Craigs were allowed to get dressed. Then each was handcuffed and escorted out through the light November snow and placed in the back seat of a U.S. Marshal's Service Ford Bronco. The Bronco had been kept running, heater on, in anticipation of its passengers.

Bruno was led out to the back of a red animal control truck. The big dog cooperated until his mistress disappeared inside a separate vehicle. Seeing this, Bruno began to whine and the whine progressed to barking. His 95 pounds strained again the leash as he lunged forward, pulling one animal control officer off his feet. A 6-foot long grab pole with a capture noose appeared. When Bruno saw the noose coming for his head, the big dog went absolutely wild. As the two animal control agents struggled, others drew their guns.

Christie Craig, seeing this, began screaming, "Stop the car, stop the car. They're going to shoot Bruno. Please, please, I can control him."

89

Vasquez signaled the marshal driving to stop. Then, exiting the Bronco, he opened Christie's door.

She came within 6 feet of the snarling, snapping Shepherd. "Bruno, stop." She repeated the command. As she commanded her dog, she also commanded his tormentors. "Tell them to get that fucking noose away." Waiting until Bruno finally quieted down, she approached the big Shepherd. Kneeling in the snow, Christie rubbed his head and spoke softly in his ear. Finally, she took a muzzle from one of the animal control agents. When the muzzle was in place, Christie led Bruno by his collar to the red truck, where he obeyed her command to hop in. She closed the back doors as Bruno began to whine.

* * *

Attorney Ted Rossi beat the marshals to the federal courthouse. Since it was Sunday, the building was closed to the public. Attorney Rossi stayed in his warm SUV watching for the marshals' Bronco to pull into the rear lot. Prior experience had taught Rossi the drill was for him to exit his vehicle when the Bronco arrived, but not approach until beckoned by the marshals.

The search of the 5,000-square-foot house was in progress when the Craigs and the two deputy U.S Marshals arrived at the rear dock of the U.S Courthouse.

When the Bronco pulled into the courthouse parking lot, Rossi waved to the Craigs and called to them as they were helped out of the Bronco by one of the two marshals.

"I'll see you upstairs after you're both processed. Just relax and stay quiet."

Rossi stood there in the snow outside his SUV, his Eddie Bauer parka keeping him indifferent to the cold. He watched and waited as his clients were escorted up the cement stairs and into the building. Finally his cue to approach came from Jack Jenrette, the senior of the two marshals. As Rossi crossed the parking lot, each step produced a crisp crunch from the skim of ice under the new-fallen snow.

"Hi Jack."

Jenrette chocked the metal security door ajar with his foot until Rossi was inside. "Happy Sunday, Ted. Follow me up and wait in the interview room while we get your folks booked."

A simple nod and a thumbs-up gesture signaled that the attorney understood how things were to be done.

* * *

Back at the lake house, the searchers had checked and taken the couple's Porsche and Land Rover away to a federal impound lot in Spokane.

Behind the garage, on the lower level, was the photo lab. A full thousand square feet in size, the lab contained top-of-the-line commercial equipment for developing and printing pictures. Four clear plastic trays, each containing a Minolta or Nikon 35 mm camera, sat side by side on top of a large wooden bookcase. The searchers didn't understand completely what they were looking at, but the size and quality of the equipment suggested the scale of the alleged criminal enterprise.

Of greater importance to the government was what was not found. No pictures and no client lists were found. Not one but two thorough searches came up empty. The search team locked up the house and sealed the doors with evidence stickers.

At the ski shop, no pictures and no client lists could be found. The search team at the mountain ski chalet also came up empty handed. Later that Sunday, Bob Vasquez phoned the news about the searches to Marshal Jenrette.

"Bob, back in Texas where I'm from, we'd say that the AUSA's case just became 'all hat and no cattle.' Hell, what a bunch of shit."

* * *

91

The interview between Attorney Rossi and the Craigs took place, at the attorney's request, in a holding cell. Rossi knew that if the other two holding cells were vacant, the outer door to the cells would be closed. Discretion and privacy were all that mattered to him.

"Don't either of you talk yet," Rossi began, holding eye contact with Wiley to show he was dead serious. "I don't know what the feds found in their searches. That's crucial. What they find helps make their case. What they didn't find weakens it and gives us a defense or, at least, bargaining room."

Leaning closer to them on the molded fiberglass bench in their holding cell, Rossi continued.

"Listen carefully. I'm about to explain 'Legal Think 101.' You need to understand the system. Okay?" Getting two nods in response, he continued.

"The term 'criminal law' refers to who I represent and not how I practice law. What you tell me is confidential. But if you confess to me, I can't pretend I don't know and then allow you to lie on the witness stand if this goes to trial. I'm going to ask you both for your opinions about a hypothetical situation. You both understand, hypothetical? We're not, repeat not, going to discuss your situation at this time." Rossi stopped, his fingers steepled, his brows raised as he gazed unblinking at the Craigs.

Wiley exchanged a quick glance with his wife and then nodded.

"Good. Now let's pretend a couple is caught taking, making, selling and mailing illegal pictures. What might the authorities find in a search of the couple's houses and business?"

The Craigs leaned close together and whispered in each other's ears. Back and forth went the whispers, punctuated by the occasional audible, "Yes," or "No." Rossi looked away from the couple until Wiley finally answered.

"They could find a photo lab, very clean and containing lots of high-end hobbyist equipment." With a smug smile, he sat back without further narrative.

"Would they be apt to find pictures, negatives or a client list?"

"If I were part of that hypothetical couple, I'd have those things safely stored off site."

"Where and how might those things be hidden?"

"My best guess would be to use 1.44 megabyte floppy disks. Those disks could each hold five to six pictures. Sore the discs inside several layers of plastic bags and put the bags inside a waterproof hard case, then weigh down the case with lead fishing weights and submerge it from a single strand of 50-pound test fish line underneath some neighbor's floating dock."

After a long pause, Wiley spoke again.

"But that's how I'd imagine it; hypothetically speaking." He smirked and surveyed the ceiling. "And if it were me, I'd keep a duplicate set of floppies, similarly stored, at another location."

"That's very creative. You should have been a writer instead of a retired ski bum." Rossi smiled and stood. "You're here at least for tonight. You'll be arraigned tomorrow before the part-time federal magistrate over at the county jail complex. I'll be there. We have an excellent chance of getting you both released on your own recognizance, or maybe with some type of pre-trial supervision. Just stay quiet. No exceptions." With that, Rossi turned and called loudly through the cell door. "Jack, we're done."

After a brief minute, Marshal Jenrette appeared and escorted the attorney out.

"You folks just sit tight. I'll be back in a minute. Then we'll get you over to the county jail for the night."

* * *

At 10 a.m. the next morning a local attorney, who had been appointed a part-time federal magistrate judge, arraigned the Craigs in the county jail complex's courtroom.

Rossi spoke for the couple, entering pleas of "not guilty" to all seven counts of the indictment.

"Counselor, will your clients be obtaining separate representation?"

"No, your honor, I will be representing both defendants." Wiley sat up straight at the defense table and nodded his agreement.

"Mr. and Mrs. Craig, do you understand that having one attorney representing you both could later possibly work against your individual best interests?"

"We understand, your honor. We are a committed couple. My interests are Christie's and hers are mine. We only want Mr. Rossi to represent us both."

Wiley put his arm around his wife's shoulder, smiling down at Christie. She returned his smile before speaking to the court.

"We've done nothing wrong, your honor. I agree with my husband's decision. And what have you done with my dog?"

Turning his attention to Jack Jenrette, who was standing silently along the courtroom wall, the magistrate asked. "Marshal?"

"The dog was taken to the county animal shelter in Lake City."

The crimes alleged were not violent, nor were they non-bailable offenses. The government could not show the couple to be flight risks. Under the provisions of the newly enacted U.S. Bail Reform Act, the Craigs were entitled to pre-trial release.

The matter was set for trial in early February. The couple was directed to immediately establish contact with the Federal Probation and Pre-trial Services officer (PTSO) at Moscow, Idaho. Conditions of their release included weekly phone and monthly in-person contact with the PTSO. They were also not to leave the five northern counties of Idaho without the court's permission. Bruno got to come home.

Transportation back to the U.S. Marshal's office and out-processing took two hours. After their release, the Craigs convened with Rossi at his office just across Fourth Street.

As Rossi drove the couple back home, he reminded them not to speak about the case to anyone else. He told the Craigs they would next meet after he had received his required discovery, a preview of the government's evidence, including any items seized in Sunday's searches.

* * *

Pre-trial supervision was arranged and proceded. Two weeks after their arraignment, Ted Rossi received his required discovery of the government evidence. In his weekly phone contact with the couple, he kept them updated on the status of their case.

"They didn't find anything that worries me. The photo lab in your basement only shows that you were a photographic enthusiast. They didn't find any pornography or any customer list. They can perhaps link you to the rented mail box, but not to putting anything illegal into postal channels."

"You're sure they didn't find anything?" When Rossi nodded, Wiley raised his fist above his head in triumph.

"Good! So we're home free?"

"Not completely, Wiley. They can and probably will still take you to trial. The allegations alone won't do your business or your reputations any good. You are facing up to five years on each of the seven counts of the indictment. I'll get with the AUSA to see if he's ready to deal. We'll see what he might offer—and then you two can decide if you want to roll the dice by going to trial."

"Sounds like a plan, Ted," responded Wiley.

"Christie, are you okay with my suggestions?"

Christie turned and whisper to her husband. "Darling, I know you won't abandon me like you tried to do, that one time at the Water's Edge. This time, we're both caught. We'll protect each other, won't we honey? Because I've got your balls safely here, in the palm of my hand." There was no harm in a girl looking out for herself, after all. Wiley gave the faintest of nods, signaling that he understood the entirety of the situation.

"Ted, I just want my life back."

* * *

Later that same week, Rossi and AUSA Callister spoke in a teleconference. The participants included the two postal inspectors.

"Ted, I'm on line with Inspectors Finch and Vasquez. Can everybody hear everyone else?" Acknowledgements followed.

Rossi began. "Mark, nothing personal, but you've got a big empty bag. The photo lab is just for Wiley Craig's legal hobby. You can try to link my clients to the rental post box, but nothing else. If you take this to trial, I'll ask for a directed verdict of not guilty, and you know it will be granted. How the government has slandered this young couple won't play well in the Idaho press. Do you want to dismiss the charges now?"

"Ted, I've always loved your sense of the dramatic. We didn't find what we expected. But I'm not willing to dismiss on either of the Craigs. However, I will make you an offer.

"It's obvious who is in the pictures: Christie Craig. We all know who took the pictures but the evidence against Wiley Craig is more circumstantial, I'll grant you that."

Agents Vasquez and Finch, knowing how the government played, 'let's make a deal', both chimed in almost in unison. "Mark, don't do it, man."

AUSA Callister ignored the agents. "Christie pleads to one count and agrees to testify against her husband."

The AUSA's opening bid was heard and quickly rejected. "I can save us all some time, if you'll accept that the Craigs are not going to roll on each other. They absolutely want a package deal and won't take anything less. If you think you've got a case against them both, we'll see you in court." The conference line went silent. Vasquez and Finch waited for what was coming. Finally, Callister spoke.

"My boss is more concerned with identifying the Craigs' customers than with putting one set of sleazy pornographers out of business. I'll recommend your clients for pre-trial diversion. Two years of supervision and two hundred hours of community service each, in exchange for their client list, surrender of all photographic images and testimony at any trials. Then they can go back to being just over-sexed yuppie ski-bum trash."

"Mark, are you sure about this? Our case may be thin but these two sleaze buckets shouldn't get a pass." Both surprise and anger were audible in Duane Finch's voice. Finch and Vasquez knew in advance what AUSA Callister would offer Rossi. The display of anger did make a nice touch of theater to help Callister sell the deal to the Craigs.

"I'll take it to my clients and get back to you."

"Anything else, anyone?" asked Callister. Vasquez and Finch didn't speak.

* * *

"That's what they are offering. Give up any client lists, the negatives, testify at any trials, if necessary, and the case basically goes away. You'll see a probation officer once a month or less for two years, pick up trash along the beach or something. That's it. What do you think?"

97

Rossi turned to watch the passing traffic from his office window while the couple leaned together and whispered.

Wiley cleared his throat, covering his mouth with a fist, to signal Rossi. "Question. Could the feds track me if I went to retrieve a list and then arrest me for its possession?"

"If you take the deal, I'll make sure that there is a clause that gives you immunity from any related or subsequent prosecutions. Just to be safe, I'll go with you and I'll retrieve the items." Rossi watched as the Craigs leaned in to whisper again.

Finally Wiley Craig answered. "We'll take the deal."

"Christie, are you also agreeing?"

A beautiful indifference filled her face. "Fuck all those perverts! You can have the list. I just want my life back."

* * *

Rossi arranged to surrender the client list and negatives to Vasquez once he had the signed pre-trial diversion agreement in hand. The probation officer completed background investigations on both defendants and found them to be eligible to have their cases diverted from criminal prosecution. The U.S. Attorney signed off on the deal.

The Craigs began supervision and within six months they petitioned the government to allow them to relocate. Their local notoriety left behind, the couple regained anonymity far away from Idaho.

The Craigs testified for the government in three trials. The majority of the sixty customers identified on the mailing list chose to enter pleas of guilty and avoid a trial.

It was not until six months later that Rossi spoke to Vasquez. The prosecutions that had come down, among other things, had resulted in eight divorces and twelve firings, while the Craigs escaped prosecution. Three days after being indicted, Gilbert Morris of Rexburg took his own life.

"What's crime, Bob?"

"Whatever the government says it is, Ted."

"Well, one thing is for sure, Bob, this case was a crime."

"Yeah, but it's a living and it's steady."

The End

Author's Notes

Idaho Catch and Release is based on a case that I investigated. The prosecutorial decisions and their impact on customers of the pornographers are true. The participation of Bruno the dog, how the crime was discovered and the parking lot sex scene are also based on actual events.

7. Father Ray

The 10-Code message meant, "All hands on deck." Ours was not a big department: 35 sworn officers, including detectives and the administration. I'm a lowly patrolman, Officer Ray Majeski.

Polk Street was blocked off at its intersections. None of our officers were visible from the house where the fugitive had taken refuge. Things could go from bad to worse in a hot minute. I was the last to arrive, having driven across town from my assigned patrol area.

We had formed up in the parking lot of the local Catholic Church parish center. Lieutenant Roger Fry was deep in discussion with Chief Lanier, so I went to my sergeant for instructions. He filled me in. Our fugitive was William Davis. Davis had a criminal record longer than both my arms. This time he was wanted for attempted murder, a federal parole violation and escape from the Latah County jail.

The Lieutenant signaled for everyone to form up on him for a situation update. "We don't know if he has a hostage in the house or if he's armed." Fry's gaze was steady, his speech unhurried. He was a veteran. He knew a wrong move on our part could have unintended consequences.

"Right now we're in a holding position as we try and get a better handle on the situation. So far we know that 415 Polk belongs to his grandmother."

A plan came to me as I looked over Roger's shoulder at the parish center and behind it the spire of St. Mary's Church. I had been in the seminary before celibacy and I parted ways. I'd also been a Chaplain's Assistant in the Air Force. When the short briefing ended, I hung back.

"Lieutenant, I've got an idea, if you'd like to hear it?" I figured the worst that could happen was he'd say "No." Perhaps, 'That's the stupidest idea I've ever heard.'

"Tell me what you've got." And I did. We stood together in silence before he answered.

"You know that would be dangerous."

"Yes sir, I do. But I think I can pull it off. At the very least I may be able to get a look inside the house. If we do have to breach, it would be nice to know if there is a hostage and if he's armed." The dead air between us was filled by background noise from the twenty cops and cars that filled the parking lot.

Finally, his answer. "I'll run it by the Chief. It's his call." I stood and waited amid the blue-clad crowd. When both the Chief and the Lieutenant approached, I had my answer. A "No" would have been delivered by Lt. Fry. I explained that I thought Father Joe, our parish Priest at St. Mary's, would help with the props needed. The Chief and the Lieutenant both shook my hand and I had my "Go."

* * *

My first stop was the church office. Anne, the secretary, would know where to find Father Joe. He was downstairs in the youth activity room with our Youth Minister.

"Father Joe, forgive the interruption, but I need your help. It's business."

He excused himself and we went into his office and closed the door. "Ray, since you're in uniform and our lot is full of patrol cars, I'm guessing that the business is police business?"

I told him my plan, ticking off the things I needed: shirt, jacket, collar and non-consecrated host.

When I told him the house number, his expression changed. "That would be Lillian Davis. Do you think she's inside the house?"

I explained that my idea gave us a chance to answer some of these questions before we settled on a plan of action. He agreed to help and we walked over to his residence in the Rectory.

Luckily, the priest and I were of the same general size. His black suit, a fresh black shirt and clerical collar all fit me well enough to pass. Leaving the small, brick rectory that adjoined the church, he led me into the Sacristy. I was now in clerical garb.

"Here, Ray," and he handed me a small, black leather case. It might have been his shaving kit, but instead it contained the necessaries for performing last rights. Inside the case nestled a rolled-up green stole, vials of the holy oils for anointing, a bible and a small silver box, marked with a raised gold cross. Father Joe extracted the silver box and passed it to me.

"For the host." I nodded and followed him across the Sacristy. Reaching into an ordinary refrigerator, Father Joe removed two unconsecrated host wafers from a plastic bag. He put the wafers into the silver box and gave the box to me.

"Be careful." He shook my hand. "Go with God."

Appearing priestly to all the world, I checked back in with my Lieutenant. He filled me in on preparations made while I was getting ready. He showed me a driver's license picture of our fugitive. Three sniper posts had been set up to cover the front door. If I was met by our suspect holding a gun, the shooters had the go-ahead to take him out. If I gained access to the house, I'd be on my own.

The briefing over, I headed out past the church and made a quick left at the corner. 415 Polk Street was in sight, three houses down.

Climbing the cement steps, I was on the front porch. I knew three sets of eyes were looking at me through telescopic sights. They would be placing cross hairs on the man I was coming to see. Knocking three times, I waited.

"Who's there?" asked a male voice from behind the door.

"It's Father Ray, from St. Mary's Church. I came to bring the consecrated host to the invalid."

The small rectangular viewing door opened and then closed. The front door opened half way and a face peeked around the door. Silently, he appraised me.

"There's no invalid here. Are you sure you're at the right house, Father?"

"Yes. Well, this is 417?"

"No Father, this is 415."

"Well, that explains it." The man behind the door stepped halfway out from behind the door. I saw no gun. Smiling and shaking my head apologetically, I stared to turn away, and then stopped.

"Well, my son, would you like a blessing while I'm here?"

"Yes father, thanks." Standing aside, he opened the door and invited me inside. As I entered, I began a visual search for weapons. I didn't react to the two guns in plain view on a kitchen table off to my right. Two steps inside, I turned my back to the guns, putting myself between Davis and his weapons.

I withdrew the silver box and stole from my coat pocket, draped the stole around my neck and removed a wafer. I repeated the words of blessing and administered the host to Davis, just as I'd received it myself so many times.

"Is there anyone else here now who might also like a blessing?"

"No Father, I'm the only one here."

I'd neither seen nor heard anyone else. I wasn't about to contrive a reason to search but we needed to be more sure he was alone in the house.

"My bladder is signaling an emergency. Would you mind if I used your bathroom?"

"Through the dining room and down the hall; last door on the left." I passed two bedrooms, their doors opened. They were vacant. I was now more certain that Davis was alone in the house. Still, there could be someone in a basement or even tied to a kitchen chair, just out of my view. I had needed information to report, and was glad that the decision about what to do next was not mine to make. After washing my hands I went back to the front room.

"Thank you my son. Please visit us for mass or just drop in and I'll find us coffee." Outside on the porch now, I paused, surveying the street. I wanted to appear unhurried as I pretended to look for 417.

* * *

Roger Fry and Chief Lanier met me as I came around the corner. My report was brief. Their attention was absolute as I detailed what I had seen.

"Two handguns on a table in the kitchen; south west corner of the house. No visible hostages on the main floor. I didn't get a look back into the kitchen nor into any basement. But there were no sounds nor indications of a struggle. Davis was cautious but not acting paranoid or delusional. I think you might be able to talk him out."

"Excellent work Officer Majeski." Lanier extended his hand. We shook hands while Lieutenant Fry caucused with our SWAT commander and the hostage negotiator.

"Ray, we think it's best if you go back out on patrol. If Davis accidently sees you in uniform, he won't believe anything we say. Thanks; you are a brave man, my friend."

My job now done, I walked away.

* * *

I found Father Joe, thanked him, changed back into my uniform and arranged a thank-you lunch for the following Wednesday.

In the end, they managed to talk Davis into coming out unarmed. I thought it best to stay out of sight until Davis had been interviewed. It was just a few minutes after 3 p.m. when I walked into the station.

"Way to go, Father Ray," was the first comment, delivered with a smile and pat on the back.

"Forgive me Father for I have sinned," smiled the next man. "Seriously, you did great."

"Have they finished interviewing Davis?" I put the question to the first detective that I saw.

Davis had been processed: pictures, prints and he had given a statement. The feds had also lodged a "detained," pertaining to an unrelated federal charge.

Walking down the hall to the holding cells, I spied Davis, seated on the cell's metal bunk. He glanced up like a bored zoo animal, tired of being an object of curiosity. Something clicked in his brain and he looked again. He stood and took the two steps to the barred door.

"Don't I know you?" My face had registered, but he hadn't placed me.

"Yes, you do my son."

"Shit!"

The End

Author's Notes

The Father Ray episode took place in California, before I transferred to Idaho. William Davis is based on a federal parolee who did escape from our local jail. Ray Majeski also made it to Idaho and later on to Alaska. We have become long-time friends.

8. The Duck and the Weasel

Today, May 10, 1978, Matthew put the gun into Daniel's unwilling hand and changed both their lives.

"No way! I don't want this. I'm just driving the getaway car. I don't need a gun." Daniel stepped away from his older brother, hands up and palms out.

Matthew Drake laid a heavy hand on the shoulder of his 22-year-old brother. "Shut the fuck up, little brother. It's just in case. Know what I mean? Now relax and let Andy and me worry about the bank." Matthew regarded the large blued automatic resting in the palm of Daniel's open hand. "Listen now! She's loaded, so how about setting it down, sticking it in your belt or some damn thing. Otherwise you'll drop it and shoot yourself."

"Matty, I don't want it."

Matthew grabbed the hand that held the pistol and slapped his smaller brother. The forehand slap spun Daniel's head to the right. The backhand blow that followed snapped his head back to the left.

"You're going to drive the car and you're going to carry this gun or I'm going to beat the piss out of you. Understand?"

Daniel nodded and wiped blood from the corner of his mouth.

* * *

The pint bottle of Old Crow, drained and dropped, rested by Daniel's foot. Drinking eased his pain. Matt's bullying him into driving for the upcoming bank robbery could at least be temporarily covered over by the fog of alcohol. Daniel lacked the confidence to stand up to his older brothers, especially Matt. So Daniel drank, as much and as often as he could.

Matt shook his brother awake. "Yo, Daniel, it's time. We're leaving."

Daniel rose from the battered recliner and followed Matt and his other brother, Andy, outside. Daniel would drive the brothers' only car, a 1966 Ford Fairlane. Originally a two-tone red and white, the Ford was now a tri-color patchwork of red, white and primer gray. Daniel was to keep the engine running and wait for his desperado brothers to come out of the Bank of America in the Sunset District of San Francisco.

Outside their target, Matt and Andy pulled down ski masks to cover their faces. Stepping out of the car, they drew their pistols and disappeared through the front doors. Daniel's head slumped as he sat behind the wheel, wishing he was anywhere else. He tried swiveling his head to watch the bank doors and the street behind the double-parked Fairlane. The ebbing of his blood alcohol level raised his paranoia level as he tried to watch the surrounding streets.

That's when he first saw the hippie girl.

She stood on the corner, just a car-length away. The straps of her backpack pulled the tie-dyed T-shirt tight across her chest. Her long legs were tanned and shapely beneath faded Levi short-shorts. The shapely legs descended into large hi-topped hiking boots with florescent green laces. Ascending from her left ankle, a snake tattoo circled her calf and thigh until it disappeared into her short-shorts. The cardboard sign she held read, "Get me out of here!"

Daniel waved her over to the passenger side of the Ford.

She leaned her elbows through the open widow.

His gaze briefly went to her hands and the rings that adorned every finger. "Hi, where do you want to go?" When she smiled the piercings in her nose and eyebrow moved. The effect was captivating, and Daniel wanted nothing more than to dive headlong into the large brown eyes that dominated her face.

"Hi, yourself. I want to go to Santa Cruz or anywhere in that direction." She sealed the deal by casually licking her lips.

"Well, get in." Daniel reached across the seat and turned the door handle.

And she did.

When Matt and Andy ran out of the bank less than a minute later, guns still drawn, they didn't find the expected getaway car. Thinking that Daniel had been forced to drive around the block, they hunkered down between parked cars. When the first flashing blue lights appeared, Andy crawled under the Plymouth he had been peeking around. Matt chose to run. His run lasted less than a block as he clipped a fire hydrant with his knee during a brief foot pursuit.

Andy fared no better. The dirt and oil on the street stung his face as he lay still. When his calf touched the hot catalytic converter, he bit his lip to stifle a yell. If the owner of the Plymouth hadn't decided to drive away, Andy might have escaped.

Neither brother ever gave up the name, or even the existence, of Daniel as a getaway car driver.

* * *

They drove south on Highway 101. The girl talked steadily about how she was going to be a dancer. After two hours on the road, not getting a response from the hung-over Daniel, she curled her legs under herself and laid her head down on his thigh. Daniel turned down the radio long enough to ask, "Santa Cruz. Where to now?"

"Take the off-ramp for downtown. When the freeway ends, take a left. Keep going until you get to Pacific Avenue and hang a right. I'll let you know when you're close," and she sat up to monitor their progress.

"There!" and she pointed to a large neon sign above a double door. "This is where I get out: The Catalyst."

Seeing an open space, Daniel pulled in and turned off the ignition.

"Thanks," and she leaned over and kissed Daniel on his right cheek. He'd fantasized about a more rewarding thanks.

"You never told me your name."

"Call me Karma," the tattooed stranger said with a big smile.

"Karma, cool! My name is Daniel. Can I see you again?"

The look in Daniel's eyes was intended to display more hope than lust. He wanted her like a fat kid wants ice cream. Was the one kiss her only intended thanks?

"Do you have a place to stay?" he asked. Daniel's eyes were riveted on the snake tattoo.

"Daniel." At the sound of his name the young man freed himself from the trance and returned his gaze to Karma's smile.

"No," was all she said.

Smiling broadly as she slid across the seat and opened the passenger side door, "Baby, meet me back here at 5 p.m. and we'll see about tonight."

And out she went. Karma gave a final glance and a smile back over her shoulder, then disappeared.

* * *

Yesterday's pre-robbery drinking was now just a bad memory. A headache hammered in his skull. He found a coffee shop and decided something to eat would be a good idea. He ordered breakfast, despite the hour.

Eggs, bacon and hash browns later, Daniel headed for the men's room. Rushing into the single stall, he knelt and deposited breakfast into the toilet. Again and again he heaved until his stomach hurt and his head collapsed onto the black toilet seat. The pistol slipped from his belt and clattered to the tiled floor.

When finally steady enough to get up, Daniel put the pistol back into his waistband and walked to the sink. He palmed gulps of water then spit them back into the sink. The face in the mirror was flushed and his sweat had changed to a chilling wet glaze.

Finally he exited the men's room, paid his bill and left. Rounding a corner onto Pacific Avenue, he saw a meter maid standing in front of the Fairlane. The Ford was registered in his name and had probably been described by witnesses. He slowed his pace but kept walking toward the meter maid. He knew what he had to do.

"Excuse me," he said. "Please tell me how to get to the police station?"

The meter maid focused her gaze on Daniel. She loved to direct citizens in need.

"No problem, sir. Go two more blocks and turn left on Walnut Street. The station is two blocks straight ahead. It's a Spanish-style building with a tile roof. You can't miss it." She smiled, pleased with her own good deed.

When Daniel just stood there she added, "Anything else?"

"Ah, no, thank you."

She pointed up the street. Daniel's eyes followed her hand movement and he began walking to the station.

The Santa Cruz police station was easy to find. Walking into the lobby, he saw chairs to the left and a wide counter to the right. He rang the bell on the counter with a soft swat of his hand, and a middle-aged female officer appeared at the desk.

"Yes sir, what can we do for you?"

She waited as Daniel tried to think of how to explain his visit.

"I'd like to speak with a detective, please."

"Can you tell me what this is about?"

Daniel's jaw dropped but no words came out.

"It's okay. Are you a victim of a crime?" She paused, waiting for an answer. None came so she tried again. "Do you want to report a crime?"

Still no answer, but Daniel managed to close his mouth.

"I have information about a crime," he finally said.

"Why don't you have a seat?" She pointed to the chairs across the lobby. "I'll see if I have anyone in the station who can take your information." When he was seated, she disappeared through the doorway.

Daniel kept going over in his mind what he'd say to a detective. The mental chess game of questions asked, questions answered, only served to bring his headache roaring back. Finally, unbidden, he went to sleep. Daniel's presence in the lobby passed unnoticed until the end of the normal lobby hours.

"Sir, wake up, the lobby is about to close. We haven't had anyone free to take your information. Could you please come back in the morning? I'm sure someone will be able to help you then."

"Yes." Daniel managed a smile as he got up and quietly walked out of the lobby.

Standing outside in the 5 p.m. Santa Cruz sun, he had no plan, except to see if the car was still where he'd parked. It was, but he left it alone and continued walking down Pacific Avenue to The Catalyst, hoping Karma would be waiting. Inside the club he squinted as his eyes adjusted to the half-light of the interior.

"Excuse me," he asked the lone female bartender. "I'm looking for a girl who came here to dance, Karma?"

The blonde bartender continued to pull longneck beers from their cardboard case and deposit them into the open mouth of a countertop cooler.

"She left with the boss about an hour ago."

"You're sure? She said she'd meet me here after work. I drove her down here."

"She's gone baby, sorry. Can I get you anything to drink?" she asked over the clank of bottles being moved four at a time from box to cooler.

With a sudden sadness that showed on his face, he answered just before turning, head down to walk out. "No."

"Sorry baby, you know what they say…Karma's a bitch!"

* * *

Daniel's maternal grandmother lived in Santa Cruz. His unexpected arrival at her door required no explanation. After "Hi Gram," he was ushered in, fed and generally doted over. Daniel asked if he might stay the night. No explanation was needed for the lonely, gray-haired octogenarian to agree happily.

The night passed fitfully for Daniel as he tried to weigh his options concerning the robbery. In the morning, breakfast was already set on the oilcloth-covered kitchen table.

"Is everything all right, honey?" Grandma asked. "You seem troubled."

Daniel looked up from his steel-cut oatmeal, surprised by the old woman's perception.

"Gram, I got involved with something bad. I was running away but the more I think about it, the more I need to face it. I don't want to be looking over my shoulder for the rest of my life." Looking up he continued. "I'm going to turn myself in today."

Wiping her hands on the gingham apron round her waist, Grandma Sarah turned from the kitchen sink and put her arms around Daniel's shoulders. Taking his cheeks in her palms she cradled his head without speaking.

* * *

At 9 a.m. Daniel was back in the lobby of the Santa Cruz police station, again having been told to wait to speak to a detective.

He spied a newspaper and searched the pages for some mention of the bank robbery.

San Francisco bank robbers foiled!

The armed robbery of a Bank of America branch was foiled when the two robbers' escape was thwarted by the disappearance of their getaway car. The masked men had taken in excess of $5,000 from tellers. Witnesses reported that a third individual observed outside in a waiting car had driven away after picking up a hitchhiker, just moments before the armed robbers emerged from the bank. Andrew and Matthew Drake were arrested moments later by responding officers. Police are seeking the getaway driver whose identity remains a mystery at this time.

As the hours passed, he gave up trying to read any of the out-of-date magazines in the waiting room. He counted the leaves on a philodendron growing in a large clay pot: 116 leaves. Twice he got up and used the men's room. His motions went as unnoticed as did his presence.

At 5 p.m. the uniformed officer at the desk finally turned his attention Daniel's way. "Sir, I'm sorry but the lobby is about to close. Nobody has been out to speak to you?"

Daniel shook his head no.

"I'm afraid that you'll have to come back in the morning."

Not wanting to be a bother. Daniel made his way to the counter before speaking.

"Officer, I don't mind coming back." He opened his coat to reveal the gun tucked in the waistband of his jeans. "But could I please leave this gun here overnight, and I'll come back in the morning?"

The sight of the gun produced the attention that two days of patient waiting had not. The officer's shout of "Gun!" came simultaneously with his lunge over the counter. Daniel didn't resist the lunge, the grab or roughly being flipped over and his hands cuffed behind his back. After his momentary surprise faded, Daniel discovered a sense of relief had settled over him.

* * *

The pretrial services officer for the federal court interviewed Daniel at the Santa Cruz County Jail later that evening. First the officer ran a national agency check to see if Daniel had any prior criminal record or outstanding warrants. He had neither.

"Mr. Drake, I'm the pretrial services officer, and I'll be making a report to the magistrate. He'll use that to help him decide if you are eligible for pretrial release under the Bail Reform Act. An attorney from the federal defenders program will meet with you before you go into court tomorrow in San Jose. You should not talk about your case to me. Do you understand? I'd like to get some background information."

Daniel nodded to signify his understanding.

At his arraignment, Daniel was determined not to be a flight risk and was released to live with his grandmother while he awaited trial. Later that day, Daniel met the officer at Grandma's door and led him into the kitchen. Daniel sat down at the small kitchen table while the officer attached the monitoring bracelet snugly to his ankle.

"The signal that the ankle bracelet emits goes to the black box we plugged into the wall and the phone line. That's the base station and it allows you free movement within 100 feet. In a minute you'll go outside and walk around. I'll stay inside and listen for the 'out-of-range' alert tone from the unit. When I hear that beeping, I'm going to shout out. Mark the spot in your mind so you'll know how far you can go in any direction. Understood?"

"Yes sir." Daniel glanced from the agent to the ankle monitor.

"If the unit alerts, you have one minute to get back in range, or I'll be notified and then the police will show up. If you're not here, I inform the judge and he'll issue an arrest warrant. So don't screw this up. Do you have any questions before we check the range and your limits?"

Daniel shook his head for no. They began the job of showing Daniel the boundaries of his invisible fence.

Daniel slowly made his way to the rear of the fenced back yard. He made it without any out-of-range alerts. Next they did the same type of distance check in the front yard of the house. Daniel was able to cross the lawn and the sidewalk where he stopped at the mailbox next to the curb.

"I won't be going any farther than this," he called over his shoulder to the officer through the open front door. The pretrial agent collected his tool bag and the cardboard box that had contained the monitor and ankle bracelet.

"I'll be by to check on Daniel every Tuesday at 10 a.m., if that's all right with you, Mrs. Finch."

Sarah Finch looked up from her knitting. "Yes."

With that he exited to the porch and went past Daniel.

* * *

Since his trial was pending, Daniel was not required to seek employment as a condition of his release. This was a mixed blessing: less pressure, but boring. The freedom to watch all the television he could stand soon lost its luster. Daniel found himself fighting the twin demons of boredom and depression.

115

He walked laps around the house. Staring over the 5-foot-high white picket fence, he surveyed all he could see in every direction.

The neighbor on the right was another elderly woman, Mrs. Rodgers. She knew Daniel was Sarah's grandson. She waved to Daniel but never engaged in any conversation.

On the other side of the yard lived a single man, apparently in his mid-40s. Slim, well-muscled and with a full head of black hair, he seldom did anything in his yard beyond turning on an oscillating sprinkler. Once a week, he'd come out in a wife-beater style T-shirt and cut the grass. Then he retired to a folding aluminum lawn chair, ate a sandwich and drank two beers.

Daniel's laps of the yard had not gone unnoticed. Monday, during Daniel's third week in the yard, the neighbor got up from his chair. Scratching his belly through the T-shirt, he appeared at the fence and motioned Daniel over.

"Tell me why I keep seeing you walking around and looking over in my yard."

The question came out in an even tone, no threat implied, but clearly was intended as a command and not to be ignored. Daniel was held fixed in the man's unblinking gaze.

The neighbor rested his elbows on the fence top so the muscles in his upper arms stood out. "Is there something here that interests you?"

"No sir," answered Daniel. "I'm sorry. I didn't mean anything by it. I'm just bored. I won't do it anymore."

Daniel dropped his head just enough to show contrition for his unintentional intrusion.

They stood in silence, Daniel looking at the ground while the man studied him. Daniel was a lamb while the neighbor was a lion. As the silence wore on and Daniel stood frozen in his gaze, the neighbor realized he was scaring the silent young man.

"It's all right kid. I'm just not used to people looking at me. What's your name anyway?"

"Daniel – Daniel Drake."

The neighbor offered his hand but didn't smile or release Daniel from his unblinking predatory stare. When Daniel didn't move to shake the offered hand, the man raised his palm and gave a slow horizontal wave.

"Hello...you in there kid? I won't bite, honest." The wave changed to a beckoning gesture. Finally Daniel took the five steps to the fence and shook the neighbor's hand. Nothing was said and all he could manage was fleeting eye contact.

"So, I see you roaming around the old lady's yard, but you never go any place; why is that?" To impart a subtle message of control, the man held his hand-shake grip as Daniel tried to pull away. Sensing that he was caught, Daniel stopped pulling.

"So why is that?" the questioner repeated.

"I'm on house arrest," Daniel shifted his weight to one leg and raised his knee to show the ankle monitor.

The muscular stranger released his hand. "What bad thing did you do?" The inflection of the voice was a mixture of surprise and sarcasm.

"I helped my brothers rob a bank."

The admission brought a smile to the predator's face and a small nod of his head in recognition. He grilled Daniel about the crime. "No shit? You left your asshole brother? That's beautiful, kid. That took some balls, even if you were half in the bag at the time. I'm Jimmy Fratelli. My friends call me Jimmy the Weasel." The Weasel moniker had been Jimmy's since childhood, a verbal tip-of-the-hat for his speed and stealth in stealing apples from a corner fruit stand.

"I never thought of it like that, Jimmy."

Daniel's spirits lifted as the neighbor showed approval for something he had done. Jimmy instantly became important to Daniel. Jimmy was the athletic, confident man Daniel wanted to be.

"Kid you've got more balls than I thought. Now you won't try to get me involved in anything dishonest will you?" Jimmy's smile broadened. "Imagine that...me living right next door to a real criminal. Hey, nobody is perfect, right? I'll see you around kid." Jimmy turned and walked up his two back steps and disappeared inside the house.

* * *

"Mr. B, this is Jimmy. How you doing, boss...? I'm fine."

Jimmy the Weasel had been brought up from Los Angeles to take care of two matters of family business, one short term and one long term.

"The Armanino kid from New Orleans is here, living in Soquel. He isn't making any moves as far as I can tell, not yet, anyway. But having the Don's son here means New Orleans may be looking for a spot on the West Coast. I'll keep an eye on him and check if any of his capos show up."

"How about the other thing?" Mr. B. asked.

"About that; these local wops you wanted me to help are pretty god damn stupid. I showed them how to rig the timing device to start the fire, and they fucked it up. Twice. So I showed them again and they still couldn't torch the place. I'm going to have to do it myself. No worries boss; the restaurant will be gone, I guarantee it."

* * *

Daniel's trial had been set for six weeks after his arraignment. He'd been at Grandma Sarah's house for three weeks now. Every week the pretrial services officer showed up, looked around and left.

The vacuum of Daniel's empty days needed to be filled. Otherwise it was just meals with Grandma, getting the mail,

118

mowing the lawns and doing repairs. Besides Grandma Sarah and the pretrial agent, the only other person who routinely spoke to Daniel was Jimmy the Weasel. They began having daily fence-line conversations.

It was Monday afternoon and Daniel was making another lap of the back yard, waiting for Jimmy to show up at the fence. Daniel saw his neighbor pull up into the driveway on the far side of the yard and get out of his Cadillac. Jimmy strode across his Bermuda grass lawn to the fence line opposite Daniel.

"When do you go back to court?" It had been six weeks since Daniel, at his attorney's urging, had taken a guilty plea to unarmed bank robbery. A presentencing investigation and sentencing recommendation were being prepared during the time between plea and sentencing.

"Three more days and I go back for sentencing." As Daniel spoke, a young stranger, clad in blue jeans and a plain white T-shirt visible under a windbreaker, came into the Weasel's yard.

"Listen kid, I got an appointment. I'll see you tomorrow," and Jimmy walked away toward the new arrival, who stood waiting at the gate.

Vincent Salemi made a point of not staring at Jimmy. Jimmy the Weasel was one of Mr. B's capos, brought up from Los Angeles to assist with the burning of a local restaurant. The restaurant was failing as a business. The value of the lot and the building's insured value made arson more attractive than continued operation.

At the gate, Jimmy the Weasel spoke. "Wait here, I've got to get some things from inside."

Salemi didn't have the status to call the Weasel by name. He was just a wannabe gangster. He knew his place and would follow simple directions.

When Jimmy returned he was wearing a black windbreaker and carrying a brown paper bag. The jacket concealed a pistol that rode inside his waistband. The bag contained a bottle of 151-proof Everclear grain alcohol, a pack of cigarettes and two books of matches. These items and some props already in the Caddy's trunk were all Jimmy needed to burn the building in a way that didn't scream arson.

"We'll take my Caddy," said Jimmy.

Both men climbed into the car. Neither man spoke as they drove; the sounds of KFAT radio from Gilroy filled the car. "KFAT, high calorie low protein radio. This is Dallas Dobro with Guy Clark and the Houston Kid coming at you," and Guy Clark's vocal began to replace the DJ's voice.

At the restaurant Jimmy surveyed the street. "I'll swing alongside the back of the place. You hop out and get the mattress and sleeping bag out of the trunk." Stash them behind the dumpster. I'll park over there by those houses and meet you at the basement door."

The restaurant was closed Monday, so parking near a row of houses would be less conspicuous than outside a closed business he intended to burn. Jimmy knew the layout of the interior well. He'd had a complete tour, personally conducted by the restaurant's owner.

With the locals having failed to get their incendiary device to ignite, Jimmy would get it done himself tonight. He would create the appearance that a transient, camping in the unused portions of the basement, had inadvertently started the fire when a lit cigarette fell onto a booze-soaked mattress.

Jimmy parked and joined Salemi in the alley. It was six o'clock, twilight, the hour at which swing-shift cops usually were on their meal break. Jimmy already had the key to the basement door in his possession.

"Vince, you keep watch from inside the doorway."

Unlocking the door, Jimmy slipped inside and switched on the bare, 40-watt bulb that cast a weak pool of light on the basement floor.

"Pass me the mattress and sleeping bag. While I rig the job, you plug the lock well with a wad of paper so the door will close but won't lock. The fire inspector will find that and think that's how the bum came and went from his flop."

Vince handed the two props inside, then donning gloves, he scrounged papers from the dumpster. Stepping down into the dim light, he closed the alley door almost all the way shut. He stuffed the doorway lock well so the dead bolt couldn't go through the brass striker plate. Turning around, he looked for Jimmy but only saw the point of a weak flashlight beam off in the far corner.

* * *

Dividing the basement of the restaurant into three parts was a cement foundation wall. The wall separated the unused space from the restaurant's dry storage area. The third space was a small mechanical room, closed off by stout wooden doors. This room provided access to floor drains, gas pipes and grease traps. The only item in the room was a single 110-gallon gas water heater. The room was warm and dark. The long-neglected door to the empty back basement area was off its hinges and leaned against the doorframe.

Unknown to Jimmy and Vince, they were not alone. Inside the warm dark of the mechanical room, the watchers' eyes focused on the two intruders. The watchers, who outnumbered the intruders, were waiting for the right moment as they passed the word among themselves to get ready. Jimmy was working perhaps twenty feet away and he'd be taken first, then part of their group would move on the accomplice at the alley door.

Holding a small flashlight in his mouth, Jimmy dragged the dirty mattress to the corner and unrolled the equally dirty sleeping bag. Moving the beam of light, he found the brown bag and removed the Everclear alcohol, cigarettes and matches.

"Almost there" he said aloud, as his gloved hands unscrewed the Everclear cap and laid the open bottle flat on the unrolled sleeping bag. The alcohol fumes began to fill the air as the liquid soaked into the bag and mattress.

This was what the watchers had been waiting for and the fumes became their cue. The assault was on as they came around from behind the leaning door. Their many footsteps gave Jimmy just enough warning to avoid being overwhelmed. He turned his flashlight beam to the sound and illuminated their rush.

"Shit!" He drew his pistol and fired again and again at the approaching pursuers.

Inside the basement the gunfire boomed and each muzzle flash printed a glowing afterimage on his retinas. "Boom—boom—boom—he kept firing as he retreated across the dark basement. Shooting in the dark, confined space made Jimmy's ears ring with the roar of a jet engine. The muzzle flash filled his eyes with the incandescent image of ten thousand flash bulbs exploding at once. Jimmy stumbled in the direction he hoped led to the basement door.

Vince's ears also rang from the gunfire. The muzzle flashes from the dark corner floated like lanterns in his field of vision. "Mr. F!" he shouted as he drew his gun and advanced toward the edge of the small pool of light. Blind and disoriented, Jimmy the Weasel came stumbling toward him from out of the darkness, still firing over his shoulder.

"Let's get out of here," shouted Jimmy. Vince grabbed him under the shoulder and they stumbled toward the sliver of light from the basement door.

Salemi looked over his shoulder and saw the pursuers coming. He began adding his own fusillade as they stumbled towards their only chance for escape. "Boom—boom—boom!" the fire from the second gun continued after the first pistol had fallen silent. Now Vince, too, was deaf and blinded by the muzzle flashes. The two crooks reached the alley door, exited and pulled it shut.

Inside the door the undulating brown carpet of rats filled the 40-watt pool of light before stopping in frustration at the closed alley door. The thousand eyes watched and waited for the two walking dinners to return. When they did not, the swarm reluctantly turned back to the lesser delights of the alcohol-soaked fabric and tobacco.

* * *

The two half-blinded crooks, their ears still ringing, struggled to hold each other up and walk, without falling down, back to the parked Cadillac. They collapsed inside.

"I can't see anything, can you?" asked Jimmy after bumping his assistant's arm to get his attention?

"What—what did you say," replied Vince. "I can't hear. My ears are ringing."

Jimmy couldn't hear the response, but he knew that Vince had moved his lips.

"Fuck me," Jimmy shouted as he pounded the steering wheel. Then he fell silent, his mind racing to come up with a quick solution. Jimmy knew the police would be responding to a "Shots fired—911" call. It was only a matter of time.

Then a faint hope came into his mind. Taking out his cell phone he punched a preset number. Unable to hear anything above the roar in his head, Jimmy started talking without knowing who, if any one, was listening. Daniel had answered the phone, even though Jimmy had no way of knowing.

"Daniel or Sarah, whoever is there, this is Jimmy Fratelli, your neighbor. I've had an accident. I fell and hit my head. My ears are ringing so I can't hear and I can't see to drive. I need help, please. I'm in my car, parked at the corner of Soquel and Water streets, about seven blocks from your house. Daniel, I need you to get here as fast as you can and drive me to a hospital." Jimmy slapped his head trying to silence the roar. "I know this could make a problem with your ankle-monitor, but I'll square that, I promise. Please kid, come as quick as you can."

Jimmy hoped his message had gotten through and that Daniel would be willing to take a risk for him. Until the fireball after-image from the muzzle flashes vanished, the faint hope of help from Daniel was all they had. Turning to Vince, he yelled directly into his ear, to no good effect. Hoping Vince could lip read a few slowly delivered directions, he spoke.

"Give me your gun." he pantomimed the speech. No response but a shrug, so he tried again, with a better result.

Next he pantomimed the words as he spoke each word directly into Vince's face.

"You." He pointed to Vince. "Get into the back seat and lay down." Vince watched and in response pantomimed an answer.

Until Daniel arrived, they needed to look less conspicuous. With his head still spinning, Vince managed to exit the car, get into the back seat and happily lie down and close his eyes. Jimmy wiped down the two pistols, including their magazines, and tried to use what little peripheral vision he had to find a spot to ditch the guns.

Opening the Caddy door, he stumbled on the curb. Remaining still for a moment to get his bearings, Jimmy stepped across the sidewalk to the nearest front yard. Bending down at the base of a juniper bush, he tucked the two guns under the thick foliage for later retrieval. Then he got back into his Caddy, reclined his head and closed his eyes. He waited for Daniel, or for his own vision to clear, or for the cops to arrive, whichever came first.

Daniel left the house immediately after getting the call for help. Taking his car from Grandma Sarah's driveway, he found Jimmy's Caddy easily. He pulled in behind it and got out.

Hearing knocking on the driver's side window, Jimmy opened his eyes wide. His vision had partially returned. The ringing in his ears had also eased and he could now hear the questions above a lingering buzz. Daniel just smiled and waited for his friend to say or do something. In one combined motion Jimmy opened the door, slid across the bench seat and spoke louder to warn the sleeper in the back seat.

"Here, get in and drive. I'll come back for your car later." Still believing the need for speed was due to a medical emergency, Daniel did as he was told. They had traveled four blocks before another word was spoken.

"What happened?"

The two would-be arsonists glanced at each other before Jimmy responded. "I volunteered to help Vince clean out the gutters at his grandmother's house. He's on the roof, and I'm down in the yard raking up leaves and crap. Vince slipped on a patch of moss, fell off the roof and landed on top of me. We banged heads and all of a sudden we're both seeing stars."

"Wow. No broken bones?"

"Nah, we lucked out there, but that smack to our heads did a number on us both. I mean double vision, seeing big black spots and our ears ringing like you wouldn't believe."

"I'll have you at the hospital in no time flat." Daniel reached out and touched Jimmy's shoulder. "How are you now? Can you hear me? Can you see at all?"

Jimmy now needed to redirect Daniel away from any hospital and the attention that his symptoms might attract.

"Thanks a million kid. We're better now, right ,Vince?"

Vince nodded in agreement but didn't speak.

"I'm thinking that we didn't hurt ourselves as bad as I thought."

Again, Daniel saw Vince nodding agreement in the rearview mirror.

"Just take us back to my place. We'll rest awhile and if either of us gets sick or gets double vision or some other shit, we'll walk over to the ER."

"Are you sure," asked Daniel?

"We're sure, aren't we Vince," and again Daniel saw the nod of agreement.

"We got to get you back, because of the ankle monitor. Vince, Daniel here is a real bank robber. The kid's got balls."

Now Vince spoke. "No shit."

By the time they reached their houses, Jimmy had formulated a plan.

"When you get home, go inside and call the PO. Tell him your Grandma needed you to move the car, so she could get into her garage. Tell him that when you were parking on the street, the car crapped out. Say that you never left, but the metal of the car must have blocked the signal from the monitor. That should work."

"What if he doesn't believe me?"

"Then tell him that your neighbor came out and offered to help, so he can confirm that you never left. Okay, you got that?"

"Sure Jimmy. You think that will work?

"Absolutely—and I owe you one kid."

* * *

Without one single prior incident on the boy's record, the pretrial officer gave Daniel the benefit of the doubt concerning the brief thirty-minute out-of-range incident. At sentencing, Mr. Hellerstein, his federal public defender, managed to work the court down to two years.

Daniel was allowed to self-surrender to the U.S. Marshal's office in two days. Grandma Sarah had come to court with her grandson. She didn't cry or speak when sentence was pronounced, and they drove back to Santa Cruz in silence.

Jimmy the Weasel Fratelli was in his yard when Daniel walked out the back door of Grandma's house. They met at the fence line. Jimmy tried to survey how the young bank robber was holding up.

"How are you feeling, kid?"

"All right I guess. Grandma is upset and disappointed in me, I guess."

The words came without any eye contact as Daniel stared fixedly at the yard's back fence.

"Are you scared?"

"Yes." and Daniel shifted his eyes back to Jimmy.

"Yeah, I know. You'd have been lying if you tried to tell me you weren't scared. Hell, I'd be scared." This was a lie from the bigger man, but a lie that might ease his young friend's mind. "Do you know where you're going?"

"Not yet. The PO told me that I'll find out when the marshal processes me on Thursday."

"Okay, you'll need a ride over to San Jose to self-surrender. I'll take you. Understand?" Jimmy gave this as a direction, not an offer. "What time do you have to turn yourself in?"

"Ten a.m."

On Thursday they rode together in silence after Jimmy tired of his one-way attempts at conversation. When they arrived at the federal courthouse in San Jose, Jimmy walked with Daniel to the door of the marshal's office. Daniel pushed the door buzzer and they gained admission to a waiting area. Jimmy hung back as Daniel went to the plexi-glass protected counter and identified himself. An inside door buzzed open, and then he was gone. Jimmy walked to the plexiglass.

"I'm a neighbor. Do you know where the kid's being sent?"

"Just a minute, I'll check," the marshal said. He disappeared into an adjoining room and a moment later returned with the answer. "He's been designated for Terminal Island in Long Beach. Tonight he'll go to the Santa Clara County Jail. The prisoner transport van will pick him up next Monday.

"Thanks." Jimmy turned and left. Outside, back at the Caddy, Jimmy punched a number on his phone list. "Mr. B, this is Jimmy. I'm in San Jose and I could use a favor. I have a debt that I need to pay. Can I swing by while I'm in town and explain?"

* * *

127

Federal prisons are mostly safe, county jails are mostly not, especially for the new, the small or the weak. Daniel qualified for all three.

Four days later he made the eight-hour van ride along with six other sentenced federal prisoners to the Federal Correctional Institution at Terminal Island. The six passengers all went into the classification unit where new arrivals were in processed, oriented, given a case manager, and assigned to a living unit and work details. Two days later, Daniel made his first friend, a trustee named Rico.

"Welcome to paradise, the garden spot of the California Coast." The swarthy Rico extended a hand. "Where you from and what didn't you do to get here? My name's Rico, Rico Bonanno. You look like you could use a friend." Rico's face beamed. "By the way, Jimmy said to tell you, hello."

The End

Author's Notes

The Duck and the Weasel combines three true events that I have set in Santa Cruz where I was Officer in Charge for five years. A drunken getaway driver did pick up a cute hitchhiker and drive off, stranding his co-conspirators. Daniel's long wait in the lobby of the Santa Cruz police station is true. Jimmy the Weasel, based on a now deceased mobster, came to town to help the locals torch a restaurant and ended up doing it himself. I interviewed Jimmy about the arson as part of my investigation of another Santa Cruz resident on a Racketeering and Organized Crime (RICO) case. The son of the New Orleans mob boss was there. The rats in the basement, driving out the two crooks, is also true but took place at a different time and place.

9. Riverside Reverse

Arnold Podulsy stood next to his dad as he did a last visual check of his work before heading home. Dad is the site manager here at the Riverside Medal of Honor Memorial. He's tall and age has only slightly softened his muscular physique. Arnold, on the other hand, is neither tall nor muscular. But he's only 15, so there's still hope for him. So says Dad. Arnold lives with his folks and older brother Dave just outside of Riverside, California.

"Please pass the carrots." Arnold accidentally dragged his shirt cuff through the gravy-topped mashed potatoes on his plate as he reached across the table. He set the serving dish down and used his napkin to clean the gravy patina from his cuff.

"Dad, was I named after Grandpa Arnold?"

Before Dad can reply, David looked up from his plate. "No, you were named after Arnold Ziffel, the pig on the Hulu TV show, 'Green Acres." David leaned his forearms on the table, encircling his plate.

Mom set down her fork and focused a hard stare on her miscreant oldest child. Momentarily speechless, she shook her head and transferred her gaze to Dad.

"Yes, you were named after Grandpa Arnold Bjorklund. He's one of our Medal of Honor winners. Your brother, who never met a book he liked or a TV rerun that he didn't like, wouldn't know."

After school Arnold often stops and hangs out until Dad finishes his workday. While he waits, the boy reads the names on the red granite slabs. Then he seeks out books that tell the true stories associated with the names on the Memorial. The stories of selfless courage have stayed with him.

* * *

Arnold believes that it's good to keep a low profile. Be the guy in the back of the crowd. Go to the library at lunch. Trying

129

to be popular is not his goal; not getting hassled is more realistic.

The junior varsity football team is a big deal, although he would admit that anyone who comes out for practice gets to be on the team. Arnold's uniform is usually still clean after the game unless he accidentally gets knocked off the bench.

Until a month ago Arnold's steady girlfriend was Carol Paterson. A red-headed sophomore, Carol recently became a school "banner girl." The added exposure was good for her, but not for him. Carol has fallen into the orbit of the starting quarterback, Bill Borg.

Arnold's friend Wayne told him, when he tried out for football, "Girls don't put out for nobodies. You gotta step out, man." Arnold's faint hope is that Carol might someday be willing to trade back down from her quarterback.

In the high school universe, there are many separate planets coexisting in parallel, unless or until their worlds collide. Carol Paterson has changed her orbit from sophomores to seniors, leaving Arnold's orbit temporarily behind.

At Riverside High School, cement ramps connect classroom wings. Between the business wing and the history wing are "senior rail" and "senior court:" sacred grounds, a cherished privilege of rank. As a lowly sophomore, Arnold can come or go by senior rail or even loiter briefly in the wide entrance to senior court. But intrusion into the court by a non-senior is not allowed. Enforcement of this cultural rule is swift, silent and varies only in its degree of violence.

* * *

"Herb, check this out." Bill Borg gave a conspiratorial nod, beckoning Herb Matroni over. Herb picked his way across senior court through the lunchtime crowd.

"What?" Matroni said it too loudly.

Borg winced through gritted teeth. "Shut up, man. Get over here." He furtively glanced around, hoping that his call to Matroni had escaped notice.

Matroni strode up and stopped, facing his long-time buddy. "What's up?"

"Keep your voice down." A crooking of two fingers motioned Matroni closer. Their two big bodies now blocked the view from any unwelcome eyes. Borg took one last look around and then withdrew a sphere from his jacket pocket.

"Whoa! Is that what I think it is?" Matroni paused in silent wonder. "It's black."

"Jeez, keep your voice down." Borg glanced around again as Matroni stared. When Matroni reached out to touch, Borg pulled back and returned it to his pocket.

Their girlfriends walked into senior court, Carol in her banner-girl uniform and Sandy in her new denim jeans, carefully cut across the thighs to convey faux age. By virtue of their boyfriends' status, the girls were allowed on hallowed ground.

Each girl cozied up to the current love of her life. The couples checked that no one was looking and then exchanged kisses. Out of view, Borg slowly ran his index finger from Carol's bare knee to just above the hem of her short skirt. She stepped back slightly from her new boyfriend.

"We have to get to gym class. Come on Sandy. We'll see you after school." The girls walked off.

Herb and Bill listened to the first bell, a five-minute warning before the start of fifth period. "I gotta see that puppy," said Herb. "How about I dump Sandy at home and then come over to your place?"

"OK, but make it at the picnic shelter in the park. I'll be wanting a smoke, and I can't smoke at home.

"Deal."

The two went off to their next classes. Bill and Herb, legends in their own minds, each had two irresistible attractants for high school females. They were football players and they had cars.

* * *

The picnic shelter was hidden within a grove of conifers. When March Air Force Base closed, its family housing area was turned over to the Riverside County housing authority. The park, ball field and pool complex, once solely for military families, now were filled by new tenants. Private aviation companies now occupied the hangars. Light planes had replaced the military jets.

Bill pulled his 2005 Dodge Charger into the adjoining parking area just as Herb made his way to one of the picnic tables. Herb waved to Bill and drew a Camel cigarette from its package, offering one to Bill as he arrived. Nothing was spoken until both teens lit up, savored and exhaled their first puffs.

Taking the object out of his pocket, Bill cradled it in his free hand. "My older brother gave this to me. A souvenir."

Matroni stared at the grenade. "Is that thing live?"

"No. It's the same weight as the real thing, because they used them to practice."

"Can I see it?"

Borg handed his prize over.

"Whoa," said Herb, rotating it in all directions.

As they stubbed out their second cigarettes, Herb spoke.

"We could do something cool with that. I mean really scare the shit out of somebody." The question hung there, unanswered until the end of their third cigarettes.

Herb's comment circled through Bill's mind. "If we play it right, this could be a guaranteed panty dropper. Suppose you pull this baby out, off school grounds, when the girls are there plus a crowd of geeks. Someone sees that black thing on the ground. The geeks piss their pants while we stay cool. Suddenly we're heroes, and we've impressed the shit out of Carol and Sandy. Sound good?"

"You bet. Now we plan."

* * *

132

Their cars, parked side-by-side in the In-and-Out Burgers parking lot, had arrived at the busiest hour of after-school business. They stood behind their cars as Carol and Sandy got out.

"It's in my pocket." Herb smiled and nodded.

With swagger and possessive arms around their girls' waists, our heroes walked into the outside food court. The metal tables were all full of geeks: four-eyed brainiac geeks; band geeks; drama geeks and assorted other geeks. More importantly, teammates from the football squad were there. The geeks would provide the desired panic. The football players would remember how cool Bill and Herb had been, in the moment. "The moment." If the two could create and sell it to the group, it would forever make their reputations, not to mention maybe getting them laid.

Arnold was a third wheel, sharing a table with his older brother and Colleen, Dave's current girlfriend. Arnold still carried a torch for Carol Paterson. Across their table and fast food clutter, he saw her standing with Bill Borg.

"Showtime!" Bill removed the grenade from his pocket. In a loud voice he announced, "Hey, look what I found on the old base." He held out the grenade. Heads turned, and a crowd formed, encircling Bill and Herb. Carol and Sandy, uninformed, stood two steps back. Arnold, Dave and Colleen, standing in the interior of the crowd, could feel the pressure of bodies trying to get a better view. It was Fred Winger, the burly offensive tackle, who unintentionally did his part to sell the hoax.

"That's a grenade, man!" The crowds' curiosity was piqued. Their pushing increased. It was coming together as planned. Now for the money shot.

"This is the pin." Bill inserted his index finger into the ring attached to the pin. All eyes focused on him. Everyone's full attention now captured, he allowed the grenade to roll off his palm and clatter to the cement slab. Then he shouted, "Run!"

Carol screamed. Bill hoisted her into his arms and started to carry her away, shielding her with his body. Herb grabbed Sandy, pushed her to the ground and bravely covered her body with his. He wasn't sure if he wanted her to notice his erection just yet.

"Run, run, run," the warning shouted to the assembled teens continued.

"What the hell?" Bill had only shouted once. Now eight feet from the grenade, he looked back over his shoulder. Arnold Podulsky was on the ground, smothering the grenade with his body. He kept screaming his warning; "Run, run, run!"

Some of the teens had taken cover behind patio furniture. No one in the crowd knew how long it would be between pulling the pin and an explosion. As the seconds dragged on, running and hiding stopped as curiosity replaced fear. All eyes remained on Arnold as his screams finally turned to sobs.

Dave left Colleen's side and ran to his brother. Carol saw the tears. She broke away from Bill's grasp and ran to Arnold as well. They were the first to kneel. Unscripted, they both put their hands on the prostrate teen. Dave leaned down and spoke softly.

"It's OK. It's over. Come on, let's go home." Arnold's head turned towards Carol, and she began wiping away his tears.

The crowd of teens came back from hiding. They moved away from Bill.

The In-and-Out Burger's manager had called the police. Sirens began to fill the air. The first responder on scene ordered the crowd to move back. Only Dave and Carol remained at Arnold's side.

When the ambulance arrived, the EMTs rushed to the teen on the ground. "How you feeling?" The EMT talked as he worked, first feeling for a carotid pulse. "Are you hurting?"

"My chest is sort of sore."

"Do you think I can turn you onto your back? Take a look and a listen to what's hurting."

Arnold nodded.

The second EMT arrived with a yellow back-board. The cops had quickly been pointed to Bill Borg as their person of interest. He was invited to take a ride in the back seat of a police cruiser, while Herb Matroni watched silently, wishing he was anywhere else.

"I think you cracked some ribs when you landed," the EMT told Arnold before he was carried away on the backboard. The grenade, now covered by Kevlar blankets, waited for removal by the Riverside County bomb squad.

"Can I ride with him in the ambulance?" asked Carol. The EMT looked at Arnold, who nodded, and the two teens were driven off.

"Why did you do it? Why didn't you run, like the rest of us?" She studied his face, waiting for an answer.

"I don't know. It was just what I thought I should do, for my friends. Because I was there."

The End

Author's Note.

As a member of the Protective Service section of the 701st MP's, I was part of the team that took the Secretary of Defense to dedicate the Riverside County Medal of Honor Memorial.

10. Fifteen Minutes of Faith

"Welcome, brothers and sisters: you are listening to Renegade Radio. This is your spirit guide, Melchizedek Moctelme. Renegade Radio broadcasts from inside our sacred reservation land. I speak to you every afternoon at 4 p.m. as your spirit guide through our daily Fifteen Minutes of Faith. This being Wednesday, Sister Sarah is with me here in the studio today for our weekly prayer circle." The voice, strong, steady and welcoming, offered a verbal handshake, inviting you to come in and stay awhile.

"Sister Sarah, what do we have in the mail bag to share with our radio family?"

"Brother Mel, I've got a letter from our sister in faith, Roberta Jackson of Worley, Idaho. I want to share with everyone the love contained in our sister's letter.

"Dear Brother Mel and Sister Sarah,
I hope my tears of joy don't blur the words on the page. Bless you both for the power of your prayers that you sent out for me last week. After you prayed for me, I was finally able to painlessly pass the kidney stone that had been making my life a living hell. I never miss your program. I also wanted you to know how much your book has meant to me."

Taking back the silver microphone from Sarah, Melchizedek hit the money shots. "Brothers and sisters, I wish you could see the hard white stone Sister Jackson enclosed with her letter! Certain as I am about the truth of our message, it's these little confirmations from you folks that really keep my spirit going. Thank you Sister Jackson; and thank you for the $20 donation you enclosed. It will help us here at Renegade Radio to keep the power on and keep our message going out.

"Sister Sarah, it's time for us to send the power of our prayers out across the air waves. Take my hand darling, so our fires and faith will be blended as I pray. We are praying today for Brother Silas Half Moon."

Sarah sipped the beer she had brought into their small studio. She smiled, shook her head at her partner, and then flipped him the finger.

"Brothers and sisters, I'm sending out to you the warmth and love contained in the sacred fire, from whence we came and where we will all return to reunite with the Great Spirit. That warmth and belonging can ease any pain, restart any soiled life and purify us for our next life. So it has always been and will always be.

"Until tomorrow at 4 p.m. we'll keep sending our love out to you. Please keep those cards and letters coming in to us. Send me what you can spare for my beggar's bowl. If you want, send $20 to P.O. Box 612 Plummer, Idaho, 83851, and I'll send you my book, The Sacred Fire. Until our next visit, remember our old ways."

Sarah never spoke until after the broadcast had ended. Arms crossed, she leaned back against the window and flashed her best smile. "You're so full of shit. You wouldn't know God if he crawled up your leg with a knife in his teeth, but I love you."

Taking Melchizedek by the shoulders, she spun his chair around, sat down on his lap and planted a big wet kiss on his lips. And so the weekly installment of their Wednesday hustle ended.

* * *

"Brothers and sisters, you are listening to the Thursday edition of Renegade Radio. This is your spirit guide, Melchizedek Moctelme. Renegade Radio broadcasts from inside our sacred reservation land. I speak to you every afternoon at 4 p.m. as your spirit guide through our daily Fifteen Minutes of Faith.

"If you are a regular part of my band, welcome back. If you are a new listener, welcome. I come to you every day to share my own knowledge with everyone who has despaired of the occupier's religions that tell us our fathers were wrong.

"For any new listeners, I want you to understand our people have always known that we need our faith. Our need goes back to our first fathers as they gazed out beyond their campfires, into the dark unknown of night. Our fathers knew nothing of the trinity or of transubstantiation. Their faith came from understanding our place with the Great Spirit. Our fathers didn't need the black robes or other priests. They knew in their hearts their inner spark, their light, was part of the Great Spirit, and that we were all one!

"What our fathers knew was lost, but it is again being revealed. You doubt me? My message is too simple, so it can't be so? But it is true. I'll only tell you what you already know, so all the proof you need is already within you. We have learned energy can't be destroyed but only changed. Our sacred fire comes to us like sparks from the Great Spirit. When our time here has ended, our fire returns to the Great Spirit. We never lose our loved ones because our fires always return to our mother. The cycle never ends, and we will never be alone. We need not cry at death any more than we rejoice at birth. Birth brings us to share this life with new sparks from the sacred fire. Death reunites us with the Great Spirit and all the souls that make us whole.

"If you know that what I say about our sacred fire is true, then help me, your brother, Melthizedek Moctelme, continue spreading the word from Renegade Radio."

Melthizedek concluded the broadcast as he did every other. "Send me what you can spare for my beggar's bowl. If you want, send $20 to P.O. Box 612 Plummer, Idaho, 83851, and I'll send you the written words of my visions. My book, The Sacred Fire, shares more than our daily visits allow. Until our next visit, remember our old ways."

* * *

The transmitter was turned off and he slumped back in his chair. Mel, or Nick Papastellanos as he was known to his parents and Sarah, pushed away from the chrome microphone stand. "I need a beer, baby," his voice boomed through the interior of their single-wide trailer. Sarah Davison took two cans of Keystone Light from their small refrigerator. "I'll be on the porch with the beers, Mel." She stepped out onto the wooden porch that butted up next to the side of the faded turquoise metal skin of the trailer. Sister Sarah, as she was known to her radio audience, walked to the two-by-four railing that edged the porch below its corrugated tin roof. She watched the clouds that filled the sky above Bobbie's Bar. The flat metal door of the immobilized Holiday Rambler opened. Its wheels had long ago been replaced by cinder blocks.

Mel had adopted the Moctelme name because it was the family name of the last paramount chief of the Coeur d'Alene Tribe of Indians. When Sarah had returned to Plummer after a two-year absence, smiling Mel came with her. She introduced him as her common-law husband and a half-blood Coeur d'Alene Indian. Their story was that his branch of the family had relocated to California to get away from the Jesuits who pervaded the Idaho reservation. They were welcomed back to their ancestral home. No one saw any need to question or examine their story too closely. Thus, Nick Papastellanos had successfully become a Coeur d'Alene Indian.

He took a beer from Sarah's hand. Foam curled out of the oval opening when he popped the tab. "How much did we get in today's mail?"

"We got $50 in donations and three book orders. Not bad for a Thursday. Remember to read the prayer requests that came in with the donations tomorrow during the prayer circle show. When do you think we'll start getting into some real money?"

"Babe, it took a while for my 'Fair Play for Jews in Hollywood' scam to catch on, but look how well that turned out. Just be patient." Nick's olive skin had made it as easy for him to play Avi, a Moroccan Jew, in Hollywood or for him now to imitate a half-Native American.

"The rubes will fall for it. Just give them time to realize that I'm peddling what they really want: optimism and a big old piece of that pie in the sky when they die."

* * *

"Welcome back, brothers and sisters, to Renegade Radio, broadcasting from inside our sacred reservation land. This is your spirit guide, Melchizedek Moctelme. I speak to you every afternoon at 4 p.m. as your spirit guide through our daily Fifteen Minutes of Faith.

"Today I want to share with any new listeners how I came to my understanding. Ten months ago I had some health issues. All the Indian Health Service could do for me was keep my symptoms from getting worse and make me comfortable. I was just holding hands with the clock and hoping that when I got to the other side I would be sitting on a cloud or maybe before the golden throne of the big old white man with the beard.

"Like so many of us here on the reservation, my dad was AWOL. It was my grandfather who helped me. We sweated every day. I fasted and he taught me the old ways he had learned from his grandfather. One day Grandfather asked me if I was ready to see some of the places where I'd been before and to know where I was going.

"We burned sage and smoked. Grandfather's voice stayed with me until I found my vision path. There I was, standing on a hilltop looking down on our lake. Grandfather's voice told me to walk down the hill and I did. 'It's beautiful, Grandfather, but I'm alone,' I said.

"He said 'You are never alone, my son. I'll help you along since this is your first time. Close your eyes now and come forward five years,' so I did as he asked. Next, he said, 'now, open your eyes and tell me what you see.'

"When I open my eyes, I'm seated on a rough log bench outside the Mission at Cataldo. In my hands is a drawknife, like we use to strip bark from logs. Looking around I see that the Mission chapel is still being built. I'm looking at my rough brown hands, my shirt and trousers of coarse brown cloth and I touch my own braided hair. Then I feel a hand settle on my shoulder and hear another voice, not that of my grandfather. The voice says to me, 'Jonah, it's time to go back to work. Our God needs his house finished.'

"The hand squeezes my shoulder. I look back as I get up and see the black-robed priest smiling. I take my drawknife and go back to skinning a big cedar log. Then I hear my grandfather speak.

" 'When you want to move in time, just close your eyes in your vision and come forward another five years. Then tell me what you see.'

" 'Grandfather I see nothing. I have no body. I'm in the light. No—no I am the light Grandfather, and I feel so loved. I'm not alone. I can't see anyone else, but I feel them. Oh yes, I feel my loved ones.' Grandfather answered, 'Your life as Jonah has ended, my son. Close your eyes and will yourself back one year. Where are you now?'

" 'I'm still a part of the light Grandfather.'

" 'Go back another year then. Where are you now?'

"Well, brothers and sisters, I was lying under a blanket on a cot inside a log house. I could see little bits of dust fluttering through a beam of sunlight that came in below a small window. Then I felt myself start to rise. Only it wasn't the body of Jonah that was rising, but it was me from inside the body. My spirit rose from the body on the cot. Then my spirit was above the roof of the log house and I watched the forest grow smaller. Soon I could see the whole earth and I continued to rise and joined the light. It was wonderful, so wonderful."

The airway went silent for perhaps ten seconds as Moctelme paused for dramatic effect. Then leaning back into the microphone, his voice came back on the air.

141

"I heard Grandfather tell me to remember the warmth and love the light held. Grandfather said for me to stay as long as I liked, until I was ready to come back to the present. Finally I opened the eyes of the body I have now. Grandfather was still beside me, lying on the blanket we had taken to the woods.

"The cycle never ends and we will never be alone. Birth brings us to share this life with new sparks from the sacred fire. Death reunites us with all the souls that make us whole." Mel ended with the usual pitches for book sales and donations.

* * *

Mel turned off the radio transmitter and left the small studio through the narrow hall, almost colliding with Sarah, who held two beers in her hand.

"Just a minute babe. I've got to piss like a racehorse," he said, as he edged past Sarah.

She turned and walked out onto the porch. The sound of rain began to ping on the corrugated tin roof. The rain masked the sound of Mel's stream as it hit the water in the toilet bowl. The sound of the flush caused her to turn as he stepped onto the porch and reached out a hand to take one of the Keystone beers.

"Sorry. I had to go so bad I almost didn't get the closing pitch in, so you know how bad I had to pee."

"Well next time don't have three cups of coffee before you go on."

"You're right; duly noted." As he spoke, he raised the beer and drank. "Have you got the book orders from Wednesday and Thursday ready for me to take to the post office?"

"Sure do: three from Wednesday and the four from yesterday." Mel and Sarah produced the glossy, softcover, spiral-bound books for $3 per copy. The padded mailer and book rate postage added another $2, so each copy of The Sacred Fire netted them a cool $15 profit. Add to that a weekly average of $200 in donations from their radio prayer circle show, and Renegade Radio was presently clearing $2,000 per month.

Just then a car turned off State Route 5. Even before the distinctive emblem of the tribal police cruiser was visible, the light bar and massive front push bar were unmistakable identifiers.

"Don't you think those cars look just plain nasty? Sort of like a stubby warthog on wheels," observed Sarah.

The cruiser pulled to the left shoulder of the road and parked in front of the Renegade Radio trailer. Deputy Johnny Weasel Boy got out. A black slicker covered his uniform to below the waist, and an elasticized rain cover protected his Stetson campaign hat from the rain. He crossed the ten feet of unmown grass to the porch. Unbidden, Sarah went inside to fetch another beer.

The Coeur d'Alene Tribe had established its own tribal police and courts long ago, so there was no Bureau of Indian Affairs Police presence around. The FBI was only seen when one of the five major felonies occurred: armed robbery, murder, rape, aggravated arson or kidnapping. The tribal police and the Benewah County Sheriff had each declined to cross-deputize the other's men. For Mel's purposes, this meant the tribal police were the only game in town.

"Deputy Johnny, it's always a pleasure, come on up." Mel extended his hand in greeting. Deputy Weasel Boy shook the hand, looked around and spoke.

"We're losing the light, Mel, so why don't we go inside?"

Sarah took the six steps from the refrigerator to the door and handed Johnny a Keystone. The three took seats on the curved sectional couch, which all but filled the small living room. After thanking Sarah for the beer, Deputy Johnny got right to the point.

"The Tribal Chairman's Office is getting a lot of heat from the FCC and the U.S. Attorney about your unlicensed radio station. Seems they think they own the air above our land just like they thought they owned our lake." Johnny drank and looked over at Sarah and Mel, while he waited for a reaction.

"How did the FCC find out about us?"

"Hey, you're on the radio. Some fed heard you or some other station complained, I guess."

"Well, I knew that might happen sooner or later. Do they have any jurisdiction over us, provided we stay on tribal land?" asked Mel.

"Not that I know of, but they do have influence, clout, whatever you want to call it."

Sarah leaned in from her seat. "How so?"

"Here's the deal. They want us to close you down—or else."

This time it was Mel who spoke. "Or else what?"

From over his shoulder, the sound and vibration of a trainload of logs filled the trailer. The three—long practiced in dealing with the interruptions—stopped talking, sipped their beer and waited for the train to pass.

"They are threatening to cut off the tribe's access to our emergency radio bands for the tribal police, fire and EMT dispatch. Besides screwing with our operations, it would also mean we'd be off the net that connects us to the BLM, Forest Service, State Police, and Idaho Department of Lands for forestry and fire. That's just for starters. You get the idea. If there was a fire someplace on or near the rez, we'd be trying to find a land line or enough bars to use a cell phone."

"Can they really do that?"

"The tribal attorney doesn't think so, but they could screw with us enough that we'd be off the air for years maybe while this thing percolated through the courts. Bottom line is the tribe wants to comply."

Mel took another swallow of his beer. "What does that mean for my operation? Do I have to go dark? Move out? Or who do I have to blow to make this go away?"

"You've got some time, because the feds have to leave it to us to find you and get you closed out," offered Johnny.

"Thanks, cousin." He knew that Johnny could only protect the radio ministry for so long.

"I'll tell the bosses I couldn't find you today, and that I don't know where you have your station. That's pretty thin since everybody on the rez knows I'm Sarah's cousin, but no one will push it yet. I'd say I can get away with shining it on for about a week, but that will be it."

"Johnny, what if I get a truck with a camper and generator and make the station mobile? One day I'll be at a turnout on Mary McCroskey drive. Maybe the next day I'd be on Missile Silo Road, behind the Fighting Creek Store. I can keep moving around and let you in on where I'll be, so you and the other tribal cops can manage not to be there. But all the time you're looking hard, beating the brush for me. What do you think of that, at least to buy us some time?"

"That could work for a while, until the feds wise up. That would give you maybe another month."

"So, five weeks total?"

"Right. Well, I'd best get back to work. Thanks for the beer," and with that, Johnny and his warthog cruiser were gone.

* * *

Sarah and Mel remained on the couch, drinking their beers in silence. Mel crossed from the kitchen back to the couch with two more beers in hand.

Sarah was the first to speak as he passed her one of the Keystones. "This is a god damn mess. What are you going to do?" Popping the top on her beer, she watched his face for an answer as he sat back down.

"Here's what I'm thinking. I'll make this an opportunity, a crossroad in our strategy. It will be a simple change of course instead of an ending." A smile came to his face.

Sarah took another sip of beer. "What do you have to grin about?"

"Okay, here's the deal. Now, I'm selling the idea that we were hoodwinked by the Jesuits into leaving behind our true connection to our spirit mother. I'm selling that we were victims. And if I can sell that, I can sell that we are being victimized all over again! Yes, I'm being victimized for bringing my faith to my people. I'll use this as an opportunity to get donations for a legal defense fund."

"You think that will really work?"

"Listen, the only thing people like more than an apology is being able to see themselves as victims. It makes us all want to hold hands and sing Bridge over Troubled Waters. We collect all the money we can, but never even hire an attorney. Or maybe we hire one and stiff him. I haven't worked that out yet.

"So how do we cash out?"

"I see two possible endings. The 'A' plan would be to drop the radio gig and get a storefront for a chapel. We keep selling books, taking donations for the prayer circle and, naturally, keep asking for help with our huge legal bills that don't exist.

"What's Plan 'B'?"

"We milk this for all we can and then move along to the next scam."

Sarah took another swig of beer, stood up and turned her back to Mel. Not a word passed between them until Mel joined her at the window. Putting his arm around her shoulder, he kissed her ear and whispered, "Remember the first of the three great lies ... 'I'm from the government and I'm here to help.'"

* * *

146

"Welcome brothers and sisters to our Fifteen Minutes of Faith, here on Renegade Radio, broadcasting from beautiful Plummer, Idaho, on our sacred reservation. This is your spirit guide, Melchizedek Moctelme.

"Today I come to you with a special message. It's sort of my own visit to the prayer circle. Sadly, our radio ministry is under attack by the federal government. They want to shut us down because we are using the airwaves without their permission. They don't want me sharing the truth of the sacred flame and the Great Spirit. Do they care that we are here on our own reservation? No they don't. Just like they wanted our lake, our fish and our land, now they want our air.

"So here is my prayer. Help me fight the feds. I don't want to stop sharing my visions, my prayers or my understanding of the truth of our fathers' faith. How can you help? They are the government and I'm one lone Indian. Well I don't care. I'll fight the feds in their courts, but to do that I need money for attorneys. In their world it's all about how much justice you can afford. No money equals no justice, but I simply will not go quietly.

"You can help by sending what you can spare to the Fifteen Minutes of Faith Legal Defense Fund, P.O. Box 612 Plummer, Idaho, 83851. If you see me or my lady out picking up aluminum cans by the side of the road to make a little extra for our defense, honk your horn or stop and say hello. Until next time, remember the old ways. I love you all."

* * *

Mel had a list of the equipment needed for making Renegade Radio portable. Generator, truck with camper or camper shell, and some form of an aerial that could be easily assembled and disassembled. He knew the mobile radio station was a stop-gap measure, so buying these items was a bad idea. A-borrowing he went.

esCurtis Williams was the Coeur d'Alene Tribe's maintenance man at the new tribal headquarters. He had access to everything and the experience to know what equipment was used and when. They arranged to meet at the Zip's burger joint in Plummer

"Curtis, I need your help, man."

"How's cousin Sarah? We used to work together at her family's fireworks stand outside Worley when we were kids."

"Sarah's fine. She's home at the trailer behind Bobbi's Bar."

"I listen to you on the radio. I like what you say about our people and our old ways."

"Thanks for that. It's part of why I need you. The government doesn't want my message to get out. They're trying to force me off the air. Cousin Johnny says that I've got about a week to move my radio operation before the tribe will be forced to shut me down."

"That's a bunch of shit, man."

"Right on, but until I can raise enough money to fight them in court, I've got to get mobile and start hiding out. I'll really be a renegade radio station then."

"What do you need, brother?"

"I need a generator to power my radio transmitter. I need a truck and camper to use as a mobile studio. I need a thirty-foot antenna mast that I can put up and take down quickly by myself. I'm going to be moving every day, and I'll just tell Johnny where not to look on any given day. If I stay on the rez, the feds can't come in and get me. I can get away with moving around for maybe a month. Do you think you can help with any of this?"

Mel sat back in their booth, staring into his coffee cup and trying to look as worried and downcast as possible.

"The tribe has six generators up at the headquarters. One could be out-of-service for a month. I've got my 1977 Dodge RV that's just sitting. I'll mount a generator on the back bumper and wire it into the RV's electrical system so you can connect inside." Curtis paused, his brow furrowed in thought as he stirred his coffee.

"A thirty-foot antenna mast?"

"At a minimum."

"There's a ladder on the back of the RV from the bumper to the roof. I can wire in an aluminum antenna mast on the roof that will be on a swivel, next to the ladder. The RV is seventeen feet long, so I'll make the mast in two pieces. The top piece will stow flat on the side of the RV. You just stick it on the front of the bottom piece that's in the swivel. When the two sections are connected, raise the antenna from its swivel base."

"Curtis, this is good, really good. I owe you big time."

* * *

"Johnny, I'm taking the show on the road today. You and the boys can check our trailer and come up empty handed. For today, don't look at the old missile silo site west of the Fighting Creek Store. I'm set up in Curtis Williams' RV. So if anyone sees the RV, remember what Obi-Wan said. 'These are not the droids you're looking for.' Thanks, cousin."

Two miles west of the Fighting Creek Store, in the middle of rolling wheat fields, was the small fenced enclosure that marked the surface of an abandoned Atlas ICBM silo. On top of the galvanized chain link fence was an eighteen-inch high cordon of razor wire. Every twenty feet along the fenced perimeter and on the single gate, chained shut long ago, were "No Trespassing" signs.

Timing was everything. Fifteen minutes to set up, fifteen minutes on the air and fifteen minutes or less to take down the mast and leave. The timing was tight, but the shorter the time, the less chance he might be observed. The setup went well and the radio transmitter came to life. Renegade Radio was on the air for its regularly scheduled Monday show at 4 p.m.

"Brothers and sisters, you are listening to Renegade Radio. This is your spirit guide, Melchizedek Moctelme broadcasting from inside the safety of our sacred reservation land. I speak to you every afternoon at 4 p.m. as your spirit guide through our daily Fifteen Minutes of Faith.

"This is the first day of our Renegade Radio Legal Defense Fund drive. More about our situation later, but right now I'd like to tell you a story. Yesterday I was in the Benewah Market doing some shopping and minding my own business. A lady came up to me and said, 'Melchizedek, I hear you don't believe in the Holy Bible.'

"Now she wasn't asking me, she was telling me. Brothers and sisters, her words hurt my feelings. She thought I was disrespecting something that was central to her life. So I asked her if she had time for me to buy her a cup of coffee and to explain what I thought about the Bible.

"I told her I believe the Bible was one of the world's great books. I told her that, for me, faith and organized religion were two separate things. I have faith and when I speak to you I'm sharing my faith. But I believe organized religions have become businesses. They have all lost their way, caught up in the business of dues, officers and bylaws.

"I read the Bible because it's beautiful and it's history, not because it's the literal word of God. Remember that the Bible and the Torah were a means for the priests, in a pre-literate world, to communicate good public health practices and the values that made for a civil society.

"It's not disrespecting the Bible to understand that the ancient Hebrews had a written language that didn't use written vowels. It's true! Did you ever hear the old saying about an iota of difference? An iota was a Hebrew vowel. Adding one iota to John 1:1 changes its meaning radically.

"It's not disrespectful, just a fact, to know that when the early Christian bishops met at Nicaea, Turkey in 325 A.D., they decided which gospels to keep and which to leave out. They were editing and improving their brand! To sell their brand to

150

the pagans, the bishops adopted the Roman day for worship and their winter solstice season for our savior's birth, instead of the correct month, which we know was in April.

"Are you afraid of going to hell? Well don't be. There is no mention of hell in the Old Testament. Hell crept into the New Testament after Nicaea. It's good branding to promise wonderful things to the loyal and foresee bad things for those who aren't buying the brand.

"When King James the First of Scotland was crowned King of England, he had the Bible rewritten. It's just a fact. It was his own form of branding, and we know it today as the King James Bible.

"We all need our faith. That's why every society, everywhere for all time, has needed a religion. It's our faith that enables us to go through life knowing the certainty of our own death, and the death of everyone we love. That's the power of our faith, not the power of a brand; not Catholic, Methodist, Mormon, Moslem, Hindu or Jew." Mel paused to let his words sink in.

"When we parted, that woman in the market and I, she took my hand, looked me in the eye and said, 'I understand now.' Then she kissed me on the cheek and put $50 in my hand to help with our fight to stay on the air, speaking to all of you.

"Thanks for letting me share with you today. Please send what you can to my beggar's bowl and the 'Save the Renegade Radio Legal Defense Fund,' P.O. Box 612, Plummer, Idaho, 83851. Until our next visit, remember our old ways."

* * *

Mel pulled the RV in behind his trailer in Plummer. With the antenna folded down flat, the view of the RV from the road to St. Maries betrayed nothing of the rig's purpose as a mobile broadcasting studio. When Mel entered from the porch, Sarah looked up from her cooking.

He extracted a piece of paper from the pocket of his flannel shirt and placed it in her hand. "Can you give this to Johnny? I made a list of where I'm going to set up each day, so he'll know where not to look." Sarah opened the list for a quick look.

Tues, 9/5   Tensed, behind the old Crossed Keys restaurant
Wed, 9/6   Benewah Valley, east off Hwy 95
Thurs, 9/7   Behind tribal housing in Worley
Fri, 9/8   Minaloosa Valley
Mon, 9/11   Hell's Gulch

The list mapped out 12 locations on the Coeur d'Alene reservation that Mel would use on a rotating basis.

"Are you going to hire an attorney?" she asked.

"Yes, but first I'm going to research whom to approach."

"I wouldn't think it would be too hard to find a crooked attorney."

"Well, I don't really want a crooked attorney. What I want is one who is, shall we say, morally flexible."

"I get it. Just a little bit crooked?"

"Exactly."

"So how are you going to find one that's bent but not broken?"

"I'm glad you asked. Is your cousin Fred still the tribal attorney?"

Sarah nodded.

"Could you ask Fred how we can check out attorneys ourselves, to see who has had problems with handling money in the past? Tell Fred we need to find the right person to handle our legal defense, and we want to check some candidates out. That shouldn't raise any red flags. If we can find out who's had problems in the past, instead of avoiding them, I can approach them."

Cousin Fred suggested the websites for the Idaho and Washington State Bar Associations. Each state had its own

152

disciplinary committee, and the website would list who had sinned enough to get temporarily suspended or permanently disbarred.

Bingo! Mel found a washed–up old ambulance chaser.

* * *

Wilbur Moriarty, from Pullman, Washington, had been suspended from practicing law for five years. The online record further revealed he had previously received two reprimands. Moriarty had violated the Rules of Professional Conduct: 8.4 (C) (Dishonesty, Fraud, Deceit or Misrepresentation), on two separate occasions. The third incident had prompted his suspension. Mel looked up a biography and determined that Mr. Moriarty was now 70 years of age. From the photo online, Mel guessed that Moriarty was probably a boozer.

"Wil," as he was generally known, had destroyed evidence in a criminal case. Incidental to a client's arrest on a possession of marijuana charge, Wil had asked to see the evidence. The deputy handed Wil the small partial baggie of marijuana.

"May I please have a glass of water, deputy?"

"Hold on, counselor."

"Thank you." Wil smiled as he took the plastic cup of water. Turning to his client and away from the deputy, Moriarty dumped the contents of the evidence bag into his hand, smiled, and swallowed the marijuana. Then he turned and handed the empty cup and evidence bag to the deputy. "Now you have no evidence," was his only comment.

The client skated; Wil did not. Although not charged criminally, his timing was particularly bad. At that time, there was an allegation of dishonesty concerning a client's trust account pending before the state bar's disciplinary committee.

His five-year disbarment had just ended.

* * *

"Law office," said the male voice on the phone.

"Good morning. Is this Mr. Moriarty?"

"It is. Who's calling and what can I do for you?"

"This is Mel Moctelme. I'm calling from Plummer, Idaho. I'm looking for legal representation in dealing with the federal government, specifically the FCC. I'm a radio evangelist. My show is called Fifteen Minutes of Faith, and I'm on daily Monday through Friday."

"And the FCC is unhappy because...?"

"I don't have one of their broadcasting licenses. I call myself Renegade Radio, since I'm broadcasting from inside the reservation on our sacred land. The FCC can't come onto the rez to arrest me, so they are threatening the tribe in order to force them to shut me down. I see it as pure religious censorship and persecution. I'm only operating on the reservation." Adding a note of exasperation for good measure, Mel concluded, "Just another white man trying to screw the Indians again. No offense."

"I see—and no offense taken. So you want me to intercede on your behalf? I do have a variety of legal experience." Wil could smell a client coming on and he'd missed the sweet odor of billable hours for five long years. More than that, he was sure he was hearing the bleating of a sheep, ripe for shearing.

"Exactly."

"Well Mr. Moctelme, I think my firm can help. Now you do understand that legal services can be expensive? If this matter can't be negotiated, there is never any guarantee that you will prevail at trial."

"I understand all that," replied Mel. "The tribe has unofficially given me 30 days grace in order to raise money for my defense. After that, they'll have to shut me down." His voice returned to an "I'm a victim" tone. "I can't blame the tribe. The government has a pretty big stick."

154

"We'll need to establish what's called a trust account. That means you deposit funds with my office to cover my fees. Twenty-five hundred should do for a start."

When he next spoke to Sarah, Mel shared his perspective on their attorney. "We got ourselves an attorney who's hungry for business. He doesn't know it but he's a mark, a patsy who can be easily fleeced."

* * *

"Renegade Radio has been blessed to retain the services of legal counsel who has experience in standing up to the government and fighting for Native American rights. He's on the job now, but he's expensive, because you get what you pay for. The first $3,000 we received has gone out already, and we owe another $4,500 to complete his firm's research and review.

"Finally, today I wanted to tell you all about a special thank-you gift we're sending out to all of our brothers and sisters who have found it in their hearts to help with our legal defense. I will be sending out the special, The Sacred Fire, glows-in-the-dark bookmark. So, no matter how dark the night, you'll always be able to find your copy of The Sacred Fire.

"Until tomorrow at 4 p.m. we'll keep sending our love out to you. Please send me what you can spare for our legal defense. This is Sister Sarah, here today for our brother Melchizedek. Until our next visit, remember our old ways."

Mel had watched over Sarah's shoulder how she massaged the airways through the chrome microphone. He passed a beer over, setting it down on the dinette table that doubled as broadcast central.

"You did great! Enjoy your beer while I take down the antenna and we'll get out of here," he said as he exited the RV. They were on the road in four minutes, driving back into the

155

heart of the reservation along Skyline Drive, at the crest of Mary Minerva McCroskey Park.

* * *

Rain had turned the dust in front of Mel and Sarah's trailer to a thin layer of mud. The visit from Cousin Johnny, the tribal cop, was announced by the deep-throated rumble of his patrol cruiser.

"Johnny and the warthog mobile are here, Mel."

Johnny surveyed the muddy ground looking for the least slippery path to their porch. Mel went to the refrigerator and removed three longneck bottles of Miller beer, then slid back into the bench seat at the dinette. Cousin Johnny took the seat across from him and accepted the offered beer.

"Thanks. How's it going with the legal defense fund?"

"It's going well. In three weeks we've received over $8,000, and the donations seem to be growing by the week. It's a good thing, because the darn legal fees keep eating it right up. "

"Mel, the FCC dude—Inspector Grunsberg—he came back. I got called into the tribal chairman's office yesterday. Grunsberg was sitting across the desk from the chairman. I got asked how we were doing in locating your station. I told them about the big push we had on, looking all over the rez every day; we hadn't found you yet but we would. Grunsberg wasn't buying it though, and asked for permission to do his own search. The chairman said, "No."

Then Grunsberg stood up, gave this 'what can I do' shrug and started to leave. He sort of looked back over his shoulder as he passed through the door and said, 'Your deadline stands. One week from tomorrow, you'll lose your access to the radio net, so good luck with the search. Have a nice day,' then left.

The week is all the time I can give you. I'm sorry."

"Not your fault. A week from today will be my last broadcast from the rez, I promise." Sarah tossed her empty bottle in the trash. The clink of the bottle broke the silence that had come to rest over the three. Johnny swallowed the last of his beer, belched loudly and slid out of the dinette seat. Mel extended his hand across the table to shake. "Thanks," he reiterated to Johnny when he got up to walk out. Sarah followed him to the porch and hugged her cousin. No words were spoken and the warthog cruiser drove off, slinging mud into the air as it drove away.

"What are we going to do now?" Sarah, her hands on hips, spoke over her shoulder. "You're the brains and I'm obedient squaw. Speak, O great white father." Her voice dripped with sarcasm.

"We'll make lemonade out of this particular lemon. Tomorrow I announce the news and add a note of desperation to my voice. Maybe I'll even beg a little. That should goose up the donations."

"How much have you given the attorney?"

"I gave him $1,000, pleading poverty, instead of the $2,500 he wanted. He calls every week asking for more, so I may end up tossing him another bone, just to keep him on the job. I don't know yet. Maybe I'll just stiff him now? It all depends on how much money comes in next week."

"But our listeners think that every dime donated has already gone to him? Right?"

"Of course."

* * *

Attorney Moriarty called again the next day.

"Mr. Moctelme, my research is coming along fine. This is a complicated case with issues of tribal sovereignty and FCC rules regulating the use of the airwaves. I can say that so far it looks like you have a very good case. You may even be able to get an award for damages. My staff still has another week of research to do. I may need to schedule a face-to-face meeting with the FCC in Seattle. That said, I do need more money. Your trust account is empty. While I don't doubt your honesty or your situation, the staff time involved won't allow me to continue. I need more money. Shall we say another $5,000, within one week?"

"I'll do my best Mr. Moriarty. Please keep working. Donations are trickling in, but my people are poor, so it's slow, but I'll think of something."

"I'm sure you will, Mr. Moctelme," and the conversation ceased.

Moriarty believed he had upped the pressure just enough to squeeze more blood out of this particular stone. He thought the bullshit about how well his research was going had been a nice touch. The truth was that he'd not even looked at the Code of Federal Regulations. He hadn't done a Lexus search. He didn't have any staff. In fact, he hadn't done anything and didn't plan to.

His estimation of Melchizedek Moctelme as an ignorant rube persisted. He'd squeeze him for all he could, and then announce that based on his exhaustive research, what the FCC was doing, while neither fair nor right, was legal. Moriarty knew he could convince Moctelme he would not prevail at trial. In the end, Moctelme would just go away: poorer, but none the wiser.

* * *

"You are listening to Renegade Radio, brothers and sisters. This is your spirit guide, Melchizedek Moctelme. Renegade Radio broadcasts from our sacred reservation. Sister Sarah is with me here in the studio today for a special broadcast, instead of our weekly prayer circle.

"Brothers and sisters, today's message is hard for me to deliver. It makes me ashamed to claim my Indian blood, because today I have to admit that the white man's government is beating our people again. Their deadline to find me and shut me down is nearing for the tribe. Before I'll let my people be hurt, I'll give up my body to their justice. Our attorney is working hard. He thinks we have a chance to win in their courts. But we've run out of money to pay his staff." Mel paused theatrically, using the power of silence to emphasize his desperation.

"We have only one week left to make our case. Please— please help us now if you can. Our attorney is our only hope. We need $10,000 to bring our bill current and get ready to face the enemy."

Leaning over Mel's shoulder, Sarah quietly gave out a few well-rehearsed sobs. With one hand on the microphone he reached around with the other, grabbed his partner's butt cheek and squeezed. A small unrehearsed gasp escaped her lips.

"Sister Sarah had wanted to add her prayers and pleas to mine, but as you can hear she's too upset to speak. Until tomorrow at 4 p.m. we'll keep sending our love to you. Send me what you can spare for our legal defense fund. Bless you all. Until our next visit, remember our old ways."

Mel flipped off the radio transmitter and turned off the purring generator. "Good job with the sound effects, darling. You almost made me cry."

"Well you almost got belted when you grabbed my ass."

"And a beautiful ass it is. Listen I'll take down the antenna. You grab a couple of beers and we'll head back home. Here's hoping the fish are still biting."

Five minutes later they were on the road moving west through the deep green of the Benewah Valley and down the grade to U.S. Highway 95, then home to Plummer.

"A week from now we'll be done."

"What are you going to do about the attorney?"

"I'll tell the old gas bag we ran out of money. His commitment to our case only matches the depth of our pockets, so he'll drop us like a dirty rag. No worries, baby."

Mel reached across the cab and put his hand on Sarah's knee as he drove.

* * *

Mel needed Moriarty to stay on the job in case some prospective donor decided to check up on the Renegade Radio Legal Defense Fund.

"Moriarty Law Office," said the speaker.

"Mr. Moriarty, this is Mel Moctelme."

"Mr. Moctelme, that last promised payment never arrived, so my staff has still not been paid for their extensive research efforts. Your deficit balance on the trust account stands at just under $5,000." The deliberate deadpan voice he used was intended to convey both disappointment and a note of reprimand. "I'm afraid I'll not be able to represent you further, or pass along our work produced until your account is brought current. Sympathetic as I am to your situation, I am in business and need to be paid." Wil needed to turn up the heat on Moctelme and this seemed to be just the right threat to do the job, and perhaps start the milk flowing again from this cash cow.

"I apologize. I thought my office manager had gotten that in the mail to you on the day we last spoke. I'm so sorry. I'm going to put a bank check in the mail myself. It's too late to go to the bank today and I'm out of town tomorrow. I'll get to the bank first thing Monday. You'll be glad to know that my fundraising campaign has brought in another $4,500, so you'll be getting that along with the previous $1,000 I promised."

Moriarty smiled to himself.

160

"Anyway I do apologize. The reason I called today is to get a status report. We're out of time. I've promised that tomorrow will be my last broadcast, at least until we get the FCC's boot off the necks of the tribal council and my ministry. Please thank your staff for having continued their research on my behalf, even with our unforgivable mistake about the check." All horse shit, of course, but any fisherman knows that you need the proper bait to catch a fish.

"My team and I think that you have an excellent chance to prevail at trial and be awarded damages. We are very encouraged." All horse shit, of course, but Moriarty knew that you need to use the proper bait.

"Do you want me to file for injunctive relief in federal court and start doing the ground work in preparation for a trial?" If Moriarty was careful, he believed that Moctelme would not even feel it when he set the hook. "That would require me to have $10,000 in hand for your trust account before my team starts their work."

"Absolutely, I can't allow this injustice to stand! Whatever it takes, Mr. Moriarty. I'll ask my flock today, right now, to help with this final push. Let's also negotiate a contingency agreement to share any judgment that you're able to get? Bless you and your staff for the fine work on behalf of the Native American community."

Mel hung up, smiling. He'd sunk the hook.

Wilbur Moriarty put down the phone and took another sip from the straight bourbon in his glass. This rube wouldn't know shit from apple butter and had swallowed the bait.

Had each speaker been able to hear the other's last word, uttered an instant after hanging up, they both would have heard the same parting shot: "Asshole."

Sarah had been listening to the call. "So, how did it go?"

"Do you remember the second of the three great lies? 'The check is in the mail.' Life is good."

* * *

161

Cousin Johnny had stopped in for another beer. He was relieved to hear Mel would no longer be broadcasting from anywhere within the Coeur d'Alene Indian reservation.

"What's to become of the ministry now?" Johnny asked his cousin Sarah.

"Mel is just going to take a rest after all the stress of this last month. After that, maybe we'll open a little chapel here in town and have regular services. He can't think straight just yet. We'll see."

Sarah knew their plan, but also knew better than to say, especially to family.

"He's going to do the final broadcast from our old studio space here at 4 p.m. today. Maybe he'll announce something then."

"Well, good luck, whatever you two decide."

* * *

The lines were well scripted. The final segment of Fifteen Minutes of Faith would serve two purposes. They would wring the last ounce of blood from the listeners and buy Mel and Sarah some time to execute the next phase of their plan.

"Brothers and Sisters, it is with a heavy heart that I speak to you today. This may be my last chance to share my faith with you. The heavy boot of the government is on my neck and the neck of our tribal council. Their threats have forced me to my knees. Better that I suffer than to make my tribe suffer. Sister Sarah and I will still be here, hoping, always hoping, that somehow enough love will come through the mail to our ministry. Our attorney and his team feel we can fight, and win. As with most things in the white man's world, this is all about the money. It's now you must help, if you can. If my ministry is to perish, I'll be waiting for you in the warmth of the sacred fire. Bless you all for your generosity. That's P.O. Box 612

Plummer, Idaho, 83851. Until we meet again, remember the old ways," he implored.

"Too thick?"

"Nice job, baby. We'll see what comes in. Moriarty won't know we're stiffing him until at least next Wednesday."

"We'll make our final decision then: stay or go. Just be ready, darling."

The log train began to rattle through town on its way to the mill. Mel waited for the noise to pass.

"I couldn't have pulled this off without you."

Taking Sarah's head in his hands, he planted a kiss on her mouth.

The final week of the legal defense fund drive, thanks to Mel and Sarah's daily churning the waters and stoking the anti-government, "I'm a victim" fire, paid off to the tune of $11,619. Between the final Fifteen Minutes of Faith and their midnight departure on Wednesday, another $4,326 came in the mail. Less the $1,000 sent to Attorney Moriarty, Mel and Sarah netted just over $23,000. Moriarty thought himself to be a winner, $1,000 ahead for less than two hours on the phone. Final score: crooks two, rubes nothing.

* * *

Nick Pappas, the newly arrived Little League baseball coach, and his wife, Sarah, had only been in Williston, North Dakota, for two months. They were new to town, but then so were most everybody else who'd come to make their fortune in the local oil boom. The city fathers, flush with oil money, began to plan how to mature their city. More police, fire, streets, parks and schools were in their future. This was a great time to be in North Dakota.

"These good people love their kids, Sarah. They won't blink an eye to donate to my program for their kids. They'll need

163

uniforms, equipment, improvements for ball fields, a team bus or van, and who knows what else. And I'm the guy who's going to help put it all together for them. It's pure gold, baby."

"Sounds like pure bullshit, my love," and Sarah paused to take a long pull from her beer. "How long do you figure until we cash this one in and blow this dump?"

"I give it 18 months. They're all hot to trot. Is this a great country or what? God, all this thinking about money makes me amorous. Come on baby; let's celebrate by playing hide the salami. Did I ever tell you the third great lie?"

The End

Author's Notes

Fifteen Minutes of Faith is set on the Coeur d'Alene Indian Reservation. The actual crime was the little league baseball fraud, which happened in Coeur d' Alene, Idaho. The story is based on what investigators call "affinity fraud" where people are victimized by someone they trust, such as members of their church group. Affinity fraud relies on our willingness to trust without question or examination, what members of a group to which you belong have to say. In other words, if a member of our church recommends something, we believe them and forgo otherwise normal research or scrutiny. Woven into the story was my own experience with a hypnotically-induced past life regression experience. Attorney Moriarty is based on a disbarred attorney that I supervised. He did eat the marijuana evidence. Cousin Curtis is based on an individual I supervised who used tribal equipment in his side business.

11.   The Deal

It was April 2015 and the cherry blossoms were in full bloom around the Capitol Mall.

"Do you know who this is?"

He read the caller ID: Democratic National Committee. "I know. Not that many people have my number at the Republican National Committee."

"I'd like to buy you a drink. It's important."

"Tell me now. I'm alone."

"This is not the type of conversation you have over the phone. Please."

"All right. Three p.m. this afternoon in the bar at the Willard."

"See you there."

* * *

The horseshoe-shaped bar at the Willard Hotel in Washington, D.C., has been the place where deals were made since Abraham Lincoln was President. Its dark wood and small size belies the stories it could tell if only bars could speak.

The man in the dove-grey suit and red necktie sat down at one of the six round, marble-topped tables that ringed the windows, a respectful distance behind the eighteen bar stools. "Bourbon and water."

Jack, the day-shift bartender, already knew what would be requested. The W. L. Weller Bourbon arrived in its customary heavy-bottomed lowball glass.

"Expecting company sir?"

"Yes."

"I'll stay at the bar until your guest arrives," replied Jack, before slipping away to busy himself polishing glasses.

165

The DNC man walked into the small alcove that houses the bar at the Willard. "Good afternoon Jack. My usual please." His dark blue suit bespoke the perks of power and influence.

Jack nodded and set to work on muddling the sugar and bitters for the Old Fashioned he would serve for the bar's second occupant.

As the new arrival sat down at the marble table, a shaft of glare from the afternoon light caused him to scoot his chair back. His drink arrived in a flared martini glass and was placed carefully on the white paper cocktail napkin. Then Jack disappeared through a door behind the bar into his small butler's pantry. Thirty years of experience told Jack he didn't want to be privy to the conversation any more than the two men wanted him there. Even by Capitol standards this meeting was private.

The man from the RNC spoke after taking the first sip of his drink. "What's on your mind?"

"We have a problem in the next election. I thought you might be able to help."

"Go on."

"It's an open secret that our cast-iron bitch has the nomination sealed. There will be the usual show of primaries where she'll trounce some designated patsies. But we both know it's hers." He paused to swirl the ice in his glass. "Our problem is that she has a negative approval rating, even within our party, of almost 50 percent. You guys will have an easy time recapturing the White House if you run anybody other than a convicted axe murderer or a child rapist."

"I see your problem. We all see your problem. Between you and me, we couldn't be happier." He sipped his drink before offering his glass forward in a toast. The gesture was not reciprocated. "So, my misguided Democratic friend, how can the RNC be of service?"

"This won't be an ass kissing session. I'm here to offer you a straight-up deal."

166

"All right, how can our dark arts help? We both know everything has a price."

"We think your side has problems too. Everybody already hates both of us and thinks our parties couldn't lead troops to free liquor."

"We understand perfectly," He gave a frustrated tug to the French cuff that had crept too far up the grey coat sleeve. "Because the Tea Party is tying our hands."

The DNC man nodded in agreement and cradled his glass. "Here is a proposal which should help us both." Leaning in, the DNC representative checked to ensure that they were still alone before speaking. "If you help us by putting up a candidate that is even less likeable than ours, then after the election we'll guarantee you the next three Supreme Court seats."

The RNC man leaned back and put up a hand, signaling a pause. No words were spoken for the next minute as he contemplated the offer, before he responded.

"You make the most of the candidate that you don't want, but are stuck with."

"And you get to appease your base, even the Tea Party whackos. You'll have a solid lock on the gun-rights issue and a possible shot at reversing Roe vs. Wade. You may even get another bite at the 'overturn Obamacare' apple."

Neither man spoke as the RNC man pondered. Looking up from his drink, the RNC man mused aloud. "We've done this before: Iran hostages and undercutting Dodd-Frank. The deal is possible, but that's all I can say for now. I'll get with my guys...and we'll speak again." Finishing his drink, he stood and walked out.

* * *

In a world of secrets, there are some circles more secret than others. The eight men in the room had the only keys to this secret venue. Two had been elected; two had been hired to run the RNC; the final four had gained access through financial largess. A mirror image group also met at a secure location known only to the DNC.

"That's the offer he made to me."

The eight had been in session for more than two hours. "But can we trust them? They're Democrats after all," asked the newest member of the group, a pipeline baron from Chicago.

"We've worked with them before on similar matters. In a deal like this, our guarantee is what the nuclear game calls mutually assured destruction. Both sides have it, so we agree to cooperate."

The leader of the House spoke next. "You have all heard the deal. It's time to vote. Any final questions?"

The two brothers stopped their whispering.

"You want to ask or shall I?"

"You go ahead."

"I want this crystal clear. The party can still give full public support to our guy, once we get him nominated? And if the designated patsy wins the general election, the deal still stands?"

"That's right. All we are committing to is selecting a candidate that is less likable than their girl. Whoever wins...wins, and we still get the next three Supreme Court seats."

"Will our patsy be that empty suit from New York?" asked the younger brother. The two RNC professionals nodded and the two members from Congress smiled in response.

"Are you sure we can convince him to run?" the member of the House asked the RNC professional.

"That's the least of our problems. Considering his ego, all we have to do is stroke it a little bit and then keep blowing sunshine up his ass."

"Can we control the nomination through all the primaries?" asked another.

"The RNC doesn't think that will be a problem. We'll tutor him, let slip a few dirty secrets about his opponents if necessary, and quietly make our preference known to the state party chairs."

The room went silent as the six nonpaid operatives all drained their drinks.

"God help us all," said the billionaire. "I suppose I'm ready to vote."

* * *

They met again in the bar at the Willard Hotel. Jack had the same two drinks waiting. The business part of their meeting was brief, but the importance of the transaction took them two more drinks and 90 minutes to digest.

"The answer is yes. We'll make the deal. The bad comb-over from New York has wanted this opportunity since Obama insulted him in 2011. He's a legend in his own mind, but ideologically not one of us. He is even more disliked, except by our lunatic fringe, than your girl. Is he agreeable?"

"He'll do nicely."

The End

Author's Notes

The Deal was inspired by my 1976 case in San Francisco, concerning a big name politician and his dirty deeds. I've updated the story line to 2016. To clarify for international readers, the story was inspired by the 2016 United States presidential campaign.

12.   The 288 Club

Atascadero, CA—1962

The hot Atascadero sun caused sweat to run down the pitcher's temples below his dark blue ball cap. Sandy and Randy made up the 'battery' fielded by the AGE baseball team. Standing in the box was the first baseman for the Tehachapi Bandits. Randy flashed the sign for the high hard one. Sandy nodded his agreement with the catcher's sign and threw.

"Strike!" called the umpire, and the game was won.

Atascadero State Hospital housed the state's mentally disordered sex offenders, or MEDSO's. The Atascadero Gay Encounter or 'AGE' logo was worn proudly on the blue windbreakers of the participants. AGE team had all been sentenced under provisions of Section 288 of the California Penal Code for child molesting.

Some were true pedophiles. Some offenders, called Omni-sexual, had no real sexual preference, but acted based solely on opportunity. Others were perpetrators who were threatened by their own desires and molested children instead of attempting adult relationships. Fear about being gay had caused these men to refocus their desires on children. Years of counseling had finally put them in touch with their inner selves.

It was okay to be gay! It was not, however, okay to molest.

* * *

Karl Magyar leaned over the trashcan and raked uneaten food from the plate. His movements flowed together in a dishwasher ballet; scrape the plate, pivot, rinse it over the stainless steel drain board, then pop it into the blue plastic wash rack.

The red and gold football helmet that Karl always wore had ceased to be a curiosity. Most knew he had lined the helmet with tin foil. The occasional, "Go Niners!" from a busser or cook now brought a smile to his lips. Crazy as he might actually be, the staff at Compton's Cafeteria protected Karl. He might be a nut—but he was their nut.

Compton's Cafeteria, located at the corner of Turk and Taylor streets in San Francisco's Tenderloin District, always needed cheap labor. Working quietly, out of sight in the back, he would have been welcome to wear a tutu or a gorilla suit as long as he showed up for work and got the dishes clean.

* * *

"Mr. Magyar, I've got to ask you about the helmet," Rich Burdette, the general manager, had asked during the hiring interview.

Karl leaned toward Burdette before speaking. "The KGB surgically implanted a battery here." He touched his abdomen. "They beam radio waves, all the way from Russia, that turn on the battery to burn me, here inside." His hand moved to his temple. "They put a little receiver in my head." Karl stuck his index finger into the ear hole of the helmet, indicating the location.

"KGB doesn't know I can block the radio waves by putting tin foil inside my helmet." Karl raised his head and pushed up on the faceguard with the heel of his hand, simultaneously pointing up inside the helmet with his index finger.

"Do you know about the Hungarian Uprising? 1956. When we rebelled against the Russians?"

"I remember it from high school," replied Burdette. "Go on."

"We were winning until the tanks arrived. So, we learned to stop the tanks. A metal pie plate, placed on top of a dinner plate, looked to the Russians like an anti-tank mine. The tank would stop and when the hatch opened we'd climb up onto the tank from behind and drop a grenade inside. Boom! Kill Russians. Kill tanks."

"How did you get caught?"

"I stopped to piss on the tank and a patrol caught me. Because I was pissing and not fighting, they put me in a mental hospital for six years. That is where they did the surgery. When I got out, your country gave me asylum. But ever since I was in the hospital, I get the burning, here." He tapped his abdomen again.

"So you figured out what they did to you?" Rich guessed Karl actually had an ulcer, but sharing this insight would be pointless.

"Yes. I learned to beat them, those Russian shits."

* * *

"I'm strictly a female female, and my future I hope will be, in the home of a brave and free male, I enjoy being a girl," sang Randy. Tall, slim and graceful, he had a ballerina's body and an ambiguous facial beauty that allowed the face to fit the clothes. Dressed in women's clothes, his public persona became feminine. Male clothes brought out a friendly approachable masculine personality.

"I've got my tryout with the Cockettes tomorrow at noon," Randy said, eyeing Sandy in the mirror. It had been four years since they met and fell in love at Atascadero. Sandy was now the night manager at Compton's Cafeteria. After working from 7 p.m. to 7 a.m., he shared breakfast and a few waking hours with the love of his life. Then Randy headed off to his job as an instructor at the Arthur Murray Dance Studio.

"First the Cockettes, then Finocchio's Review, darling." The Cockettes were San Francisco's 'entry level' drag queen dance company. But unlike the Rockettes, the Cockettes were drag queens, some bearded and all flamboyant.

Finocchio's in San Francisco's North Beach was a fun, high-class club where all segments of the community, straight, gay,

172

black or white, could mix and enjoy beautiful talented female impersonation artists.

* * *

Sally Roxanne sat alone at a table in the back corner of Compton's nursing a cup of tomato soup. Her long sleeves covered tattoos that would detract from her efforts to cross-dress. She'd fixed soup by adding catsup to a cup of hot water she served herself from the urn next to the two large coffee pots. It was 1:30 a.m. and Sally lacked the price of a meal. The soup she made would have to do. Sometimes one of the other drag queens that came in after the bars closed bought her a meal.

Sally, named Walter at birth, had been a merchant seaman. Walter lost his maritime ticket after being convicted of raping a 15-year-old girl. The facts that the girl was a hooker and looked 20 were not persuasive to the judge. Fearing her pimp, the girl had cried rape and sacrificed him rather than face a beating. He ended up at Atascadero State Hospital for treatment, since he wore the twin labels of rapist and child molester.

Released from Atascadero at age 59 with no skills and no support, he adopted the name Sally and became one of the Tenderloin's subsistence sex workers.

Today was Sally's 60th birthday. A single thought kept filling her mind. The only thing worse than being a whore is being an old whore. Crumbling a package of saltine crackers into the soup, she wet a fingertip and mopped up the few crumbs that had missed the cup. Sally knew her welcome in Compton's hung by the slender thread of the shift manager's kindness.

"Happy birthday, Sally!" Sandy set down the plate. A hot turkey sandwich and a scoop of mashed potatoes sat there, both smothered in translucent beige gravy. His other hand set down a second plate. An iced cupcake with a single pink candle centered amid multicolored sprinkles that flecked the white icing.

A small crowd consisting of cooks, waitresses and Karl joined Sandy and formed a loose semi-circle in front of the table. When a ragged chorus of "Happy Birthday" broke out, Sally began to cry.

Sandy patted Sally gently on the shoulder and quietly removed the cup of ersatz soup.

Wiping her eyes, Sally managed to smear her eye make-up out and up, as if she had done the work deliberately for a part in "The Mikado."

The song concluded and everybody offered final birthday wishes and went back to work. Sally was surprised, not so much that they knew of her birthday, but that anybody cared.

"See you at home," said Karl, before going back to his station at the dish sink.

* * *

Months ago, Karl had noticed Sally sitting in her usual corner at Compton's. He'd offered her his couch and she'd accepted. Sally had assumed she was being offered a trade–shelter for sex–and had been surprised when Karl asked nothing in return.

Their two-room flat was just down the block from Compton's. On her first night there, Sally had been confronted with two surprises. First, Karl's mattress was on the floor beneath a scarred oak dining room table.

"The KGB put a radio receiver in my head, and they send radio waves that burn me—here," and Karl tapped his abdomen. "The table blocks the waves when I take my helmet off at night." Sally just nodded and smiled.

The second surprise came without warning. On top of the table under which Karl slept was a large fish bowl. Peeking over the edge of the bowl, perhaps about to make an exit, was a large yellow banana slug.

"Shit! Karl there's a slug in here for Christ sake. Do something!"

"That's my pet. His name is Sluggo. Just look at his little slug mug, cute huh? He's quiet and really quite affectionate, once he got to know me. He won't bother you, and he stays pretty much around his little house."

Karl's assurance had not stopped Sally from sleeping uneasily. Eventually, Sally had moved from the couch to Karl's bed, and their relationship matured from one of convenience toward a partnership or perhaps even true love.

* * *

The 288 Club—at 288 Turk Street—was run by Tommy Dragovich, or 'Tenderloin Tommy,' as he was known in the neighborhood. The Tenderloin's sex workers—straight, gay or the colorful trannies, also frequented Tommy's bar. The inside joke among the patrons and the cops was that you had to have a 288 PC conviction to be allowed inside.

Tommy used his bar as the headquarters for his many businesses; loan sharking, gambling, drugs and prostitution.

During the summer of 1966, profits from prostitution were down, a casualty of the free love movement of the hippies. The drug trade was also in a slump. The Hell's Angels had staked a claim to moving drugs in the Haight-Ashbury district. The Black Guerrilla Family wanted the black drug market exclusively for their dealers.

Tommy felt squeezed, and he didn't like it. He pushed back by roughly smacking any hands he felt were reaching into his rice bowl. The Hell's Angels were well armed, as were the street-wise black dealers. So, he and his hulking enforcer

Gundar, known on the street as 'Gundar the Barbarian,' chose to concentrate on consolidating his monopoly on prostitution in the Tenderloin.

Young boys, underage girls, professional sex workers of either gender or any age were all just commodities to Tommy. He considered himself nothing more than a broker, an arranger between willing buyers and sellers.

The word went out on the street telegraph. Check in with Tommy at the 288 Club. And check in they did.

"I'm not your pimp. I don't love you. I won't protect you or pay your bail. What I am is your landlord, plain and simple. I make this simple for both of us. Your rent is a flat $20 a day, seven days a week. When you work and what you make is up to you. I hope you make a million bucks. Just pay your rent. Simple!"

"Gundar is going to put your name in his book and your face in his memory." Gundar's visage showed neither a smile nor grimace, but his silence and appearance spoke volumes.

"What if I can't pay?" a few asked.

"Good question," replied Tommy. "In that case, you can get out of my neighborhood and never come back."

"If I don't?" someone asked Tommy, who kept smiling as he leaned forward conspiratorially. "You really don't want to know. Let's just say, nothing good. Now go see Gundar and get to work."

* * *

Sally Roxanne heard the word and got the talk from Tommy. She was powerless, and did what she was told—by her customers and by Tommy. The rent was just another form of rape, and she was used to that by now. She knew she was old, and that she subsisted on the scraps of her trade. Sally survived on cheap sex with punks and perverts, hidden in

176

alleys and behind trash bins. She handled all the people no self-respecting whore would touch.

Gundar kept the book, tracking what each whore owed and when they paid. He never threatened, thanked or even acknowledged their payments. He just took. It was August 15 when Sally showed up for her last weekly.

"I don't have all my rent," she said, her eyes downcast.

Gundar didn't speak, but instantly his right hand curled into a fist that struck out and caught Sally at the jaw line, knocking her flat. He stood silently, his eyes never leaving Sally as she got up from the floor.

"That's the warning. That's me saying, 'please.' Have Tommy's money tomorrow. I won't be saying 'please' next time."

That was it.

When Tommy came into his bar later that day, Gundar told him about Sally's failure to pay. Next he mentioned the deadline he'd issued.

"She isn't the first tranny to pull this shit?"

"No boss. They're all pushing the limits on paying."

"If she doesn't pay tomorrow, make an example of her. Send a message. Know what I mean?'

"Yes, boss."

"Put Sally one step closer to being a real split-tail. You know what to do." Tommy didn't get a response from the big man, just a small nod. Gundar knew what to do.

* * *

Sally mentioned the unpaid rent, the punch and the deadline to Karl. She'd hide out at home for a couple of days and then figure out what to do. She had no plan beyond hiding.

When Sally failed to show up, Gundar began to ask around. Where did she live? Who, if anyone, with power did she know?

The answers came quickly from some of Tommy's girls. The small apartment where Sally was hiding was just half-way down the block from the bar, and crazy Karl seemed to be her only friend. Gundar planned his visit for that night while Karl was at work. He saw no need to come during the day and mess up Karl just because he happened to be at home when Sally got her visit.

The small brass name slot on the scarred door read 'Magyar.' With his ear to the door, Gundar could tell someone was inside. He knocked softly. The soft knock did the trick. Sally spoke through the door.

"Who's there?"

"Building super; I've got a telegram for Karl."

"Just slide it under the door please. I'm not dressed. "

"Can't. Someone has to sign, to confirm delivery."

The door opened several inches with only Sally's face visible past the edge. Gundar didn't wait for her to speak. He grabbed her by the hair with one huge hand while leaning into the door. His great bulk forced the door open and he backed her into the apartment. He kept advancing and she kept backing up, until Sally fell onto the couch when Gundar's first punch landed.

"Now I'm going to get into your pants!" was the last thing Sally heard before she blacked out from the second blow.

He's going to rape me, she thought, just before her mind went black.

When Sally awoke, on the edge of consciousness while her mind still floated, searching for reality, there was a dull pain down there, somewhere near her lap. The pain focused her wakefulness as the haze lifted from her mind. She saw that she was naked from the waist down. There was her penis, intact and resting above two red ovals that dangled several inches down by slender blue-white cords. Focusing on the pain, her hands moved to her lap, pushing the flaccid penis aside. There was blood on her thighs and on the couch. The sight of her

178

scrotum, cleanly sliced in two—her testicles, hanging by their sperm ducts—brought forth her screams. How long she screamed she didn't know as her mind returned to black.

Gundar was quiet as he stood behind the heavy oak table that covered Karl and Sally's dining room floor and bedding. After slitting Sally's bag he'd casually been exploring the apartment.

Sluggo had taken himself out for a walk across the tabletop, until it was cut short by the fall of Gundar's hand. Sluggo began to curl into a protective ball at the first touch. Gundar felt the soft mass and raised his hand. What he saw made the big man jump back and curse, shaking his hand and looking for something to wipe off Sluggo's slime. He grabbed a handful of bedding from beneath the table. Stepping into what passed for a kitchen Gundar washed his hands and began searching. He found a paring knife in the dish drainer by the sink. Returning to the table, he slammed the point of the blade through Sluggo's soft body, pinning the slug to the table top. Sluggo writhed and flexed his body, all to no avail. Gundar watched, until finally Karl's pet became still.

Randy was taking a bubble bath in celebration of getting hired for Finocchio's new review. On a whim, he decided to share the good news with Sally if she was home. Wrapping himself in a towel and stepping into slippers, Randy was at Karl and Sally's door in less than two minutes. The door was unlocked, so he went inside.

Straight ahead lay Sally, legs spread, still bleeding from the attack. In four steps Randy was across the room, kneeling in front of her, trying to think of what to do. From the pain or the sight of damage, Sally was still unconscious.

Randy had not noticed Gundar's quiet form. Kneeling before the maimed Sally, Randy's long black hair—still wet from the bath—hung down over his narrow shoulders. Gundar had seen Randy several times at Compton's after the 288 Club had closed at 2 a.m. He always thought Randy was just another of the transvestites who gathered at Compton's most nights.

Unknown to Gundar was that Randy came in to see his partner Sandy, and not just to dish with the girls.

Slipping out of the apartment behind the kneeling figure seemed risky to the big man. Besides, this was just another queen, which marked Randy as a lower order of life in Gundar's mind. Not a thinker by nature, he made his choice. Violence had always worked before, so it came easily to him now.

Rocking the paring knife blade free from the table top, he flicked Sluggo's skewered body to the floor. It landed with a soft thud. In three steps, Gundar was behind Randy. It was quick because there was no hesitation, just purposeful violence. He grabbed a handful of the long wet hair, jerked back Randy's head and cut his throat in one motion, deep and swift. With the black hair held in one hand, he grabbed the side of Randy's head, keeping him upright without inflicting any suspicious bruises. As the liquid life flowed away, Randy tried to move, to resist, and to cover the gaping wound. Nothing worked as the big man held fast and blood soaked the front of the bath towel that was Randy's only cover.

With Randy forever stilled, Gundar left him posed on his knees in front of Sally. He finished his work by completing the small tableau. To the cops, he presented a plausible murder-suicide, or, if they preferred, the equally possible lover's quarrel gone bad. Moving to the outside of Sally's position on the couch, he used the knife again, cutting her femoral artery, high up on the inside of her thigh. Bright red arterial blood began to pulse out from the single cut, soaking his two victims and combining into one final pool that spread under the couch and around the feet and legs of the bodies. Carefully, he wiped the handle of the knife with his handkerchief, removing his own prints, before pressing it into Randy's hand, then letting it fall flat into the pool of blood. He knew that the scene would speak for itself. His work done, he left, wiping any spots on the door that he may have touched.

* * *

Sandy saw the police cruisers and then the coroner's van arrive. The police, and even dead bodies, were common fare in the Tenderloin, so he didn't pay much attention. He kept working, not having time for someone else's trouble.

Upstairs in Karl's building, the sea of blue uniforms and the coroner had been joined by two detectives. The senior detective, Don Fagetti, stood just inside the doorway of the small apartment and spoke to the patrolman who controlled the door.

"What have we got?"

"TFB—typical faggot beef. Misdemeanor homicides," replied the cop, who let the detectives enter.

Fagetti's partner, Jerry Frimmersdorf, stepped around Fagetti to get a closer look at the crime scene.

"Jesus. Why is it that these people are so fond of blades? Knives, straight razors—you'd think they'd use a gun like the rest of the scumbags. What a mess."

"The blood seeped through the ceiling of the apartment downstairs and scared the shit out of the old broad below," advised the cop that got the initial call. Fagetti and Frimmersdorf surveyed the scene over the back of a kneeling photographer. "What do you think, Jerry? The young one is blowing the old one and it goes wrong? Black hair cuts the gray hair's bag because he's pissed off. Gray hair goes ape shit and cuts Blackie's throat?"

"Man, I don't know. I don't care who is sucking or cutting who. Do we really need to know? We got the knife, the cuts, no sign of restraint or struggle and no forced entry. I think the scene kind of speaks for itself. I say we release the bodies after the techs finish, wait to see if we've got any unexplained prints and go from there."

"Inspectors, we've got something I want you to see, over here in the corner," advised another cop who was checking around inside the apartment.

181

Fagetti left his partner and walked across the room to where the cop was pointing down to something shriveled on the floor. It was Sluggo.

"Shit, it looks like—," but Fagetti's words failed him.

"A dead banana slug? Maybe it's a new queer thing, banana slug up the ass, like they do with the gerbils," speculated the cop.

"Weird shit, no doubt. Make sure that the tech gets a picture, then bag it and tag it." Fagetti rejoined his partner and filled him in on the dead slug, adding to the bizarreness of the scene.

* * *

"Sandy, you'd better go on home," Betty, one of his wait staff, whispered into his ear. "They just took two gurneys into your building. Go check, honey. I'll cover."

When he reached the third floor, Sandy saw that the police were inside his neighbor's apartment. Secretly, he was glad that whatever bad thing had happened was next door and not at his place. As he reached for his doorknob a cop looked out from Karl's door and spoke.

"Hey."

Sandy nodded to acknowledge.

"Would you mind taking a look, to see if you can identify either of the victims?" Sandy's ears locked on the plural use of the word as he walked the few steps down the hall.

"Inspector, I've got the neighbor here. Do you want him to attempt an ID?"

Fagetti nodded affirmatively and stood up to meet the stranger at the door.

"I'm Inspector Fagetti and that's Inspector Frimmersdorf, my partner. Who are you?"

"I'm Sandy Silva. I live next door."

"Can you tell me who lives here?"

"Karl Magyar, who works for me at Compton's, and his partner Sally—uh—Walter."

"This is a mess. It would help us if you'd take a look and tell me if you recognize either of the two men."

"I'd be glad to," replied Sandy, as the inspector's words, 'two men,' echoed in his mind.

"Stay with me and don't touch anything. Just tell me if you recognize anyone." Fagetti turned and led Sandy across the room to the left rear of the two bodies. Looking over Frimmersdorf's shoulders, Sandy let out an audible gasp as his worst fears were confirmed. Fagetti couldn't decide if Sandy was fainting or lunging when he fell onto Frimmersdorf's back. Fagetti and Frimmersdorf had long ago become immune to the impact of the blood and violence at crime scenes. Fagetti hadn't been prepared for Sandy's response. He grabbed him around the shoulders, pinning his arms back, all the while supporting his dead weight.

In Fagetti's firm hold, Sandy stopped. Suddenly his vision went to black in the temporary oblivion of unconsciousness. He awoke to find himself on the floor. The two detectives were above him. Fagetti kneeled and offered him a glass of water.

"Who are they, Mr. Silva?"

Sandy opened his mouth to speak, but no sound emerged. Fagetti pushed the water forward and Sandy drank.

"On the couch is W-Walter, Karl's partner, he goes by Sally. The young man on his knees is Randy Fernelius, m-my partner."

The two detectives exchanged glances while helping Sandy to his feet.

"Is there somebody you'd like me to call for you?"

"No, I've got to go back to work at Compton's. I'm the night manager." The words came out flat with neither tone nor inflection.

"That's not a good idea, Mr. Silva. I'll go down to the cafeteria and take care of it. You should go home now. Please. I'll check in with you tomorrow, and we'll talk more then."

There was true concern in Fagetti's voice. He could still feel the emotions of victims, even though he had long since stopped reacting to the terrible scenes. Sandy did as he was told, going inside and silently closing his door, the better to weep in private.

* * *

Back down stairs in Compton's, Inspector Fagetti walked to the cash register, showed his badge and told the waitress that he needed to see the on-duty manager.

"Well, you're in luck handsome, that would be me," offered Betty.

"Two things, darling, Mr. Silva won't be back tonight. There was a problem."

"No worries, we'll make do."

"And I need Karl Magyar. Could you get him for me, please?"

"Another problem?" Betty asked. Fagetti gave a slow affirmative nod.

"I'll send him out. Will he be back tonight?"

This time Fagetti shook his head. Karl emerged from the back, still wearing his black rubberized apron, gloves and helmet. Very little shocked or surprised Fagetti anymore, but seeing the football helmet stopped him in his tracks. Fagetti again showed his badge and spoke softly to the helmeted dishwasher. Betty hung back, not wanting to intrude. Karl handed her his apron and gloves, then followed the inspector to a table in the corner where Jerry Frimmersdorf sat.

Compton's was not the best place to talk, thought Fagetti, but the police station would be worse and the apartment was still a crime scene. The bodies would be gone when Karl finally

184

got home, but the gore at the scene would be a terrible greeting. Tomorrow he could contact Reverend Williams at the Glide Memorial Church. Residents of the Tenderloin were the Rev's flock, and volunteers from Glide could clean the apartment. Whether through sympathy or empathy, he thought that sparing Karl the everlasting image of the blood and what the poses of the victims suggested, was the least he could do.

"Can I call you Karl?"

The inspector got an affirmative nod back.

"Karl, I've got nothing you want to hear. Someone got into your apartment and killed your partner, Walter. I'm very sorry."

The three men sat in silence as the background noise of the cafeteria filled the moment. While the seconds dragged on, Karl neither spoke nor responded, as the two detectives exchanged glances.

"Listen Karl, you're not able to go back to your apartment tonight, as our people are processing the scene for evidence. We're going to drive you to the Whitman Hotel on Market Street and get you a room for the night. The city will pay, and the hotel keeps small toiletry kits for the guests that we bring in. Jerry and I will come back and get you tomorrow. Then we'll go downtown and talk. We need your help to figure out who killed Walter. Come on, it's late."

Fagetti and Frimmerdorf rose from their seats and Karl followed. Silently, they went out to the double-parked police sedan. At the hotel, Fagetti walked Karl into the deserted lobby and hit the bell on the counter to summon a clerk. Emerging from a doorway, the clerk tried to look alert for the customers. Fagetti showed his badge and asked for a SFPD housing voucher, which he signed.

"Can I have a room with a big wood table please? At home I sleep under my table." Karl stopped, not wanting to share his reason.

Fagetti looked to the hotel clerk. "You got a room with a table?" The clerk shook his head. The answer upset Karl who leaned in to whisper in the detective's ear.

"I have enemies. They burn me with invisible waves when I take the helmet off. Table blocks the waves."

Nodding to show he understood, Fagetti whispered back. "I've seen this before. I understand," and he looked around conspiratorially before going on. "Sleep in the steel bath with your head below the rim. It works—I know." Fagetti's answer, coupled with his delivery, satisfied Karl, who nodded in agreement. Then Fagetti turned back to the desk clerk.

"One night, please, and Karl will need one of your overnight kits."

"We'll come pick you up, here in the lobby at 9 a.m. tomorrow, Karl. We'll get some breakfast and then go to the station."

Karl just nodded in reply and Fagetti patted his shoulder before he walked out. Fagetti was used to the long days that went with the job. It was just past 1:30 a.m., and breakfast at 9 a.m. would come too soon.

* * *

The double murders of Sally and Randy, minus most of the sensational details, made the interior of the papers. The police knew not to reveal details of a crime scene that could only be known to the perpetrator. Regardless, they could always count on having one or more nuts walk in and confess to the crime. If the intimate details of the crime became public knowledge, it became harder to separate the guilty from the crazy. Or, as some of the homicide squad joked, "find out who tried to separate the fruit from his nuts."

The interview with Karl did little to advance the investigation. Karl told them about the payment demand Sally had received from Gundar. He had nothing more. When asked

186

about the dead gastropod, he began to cry. As the two detectives exchanged glances, Karl explained about his pet, Sluggo. Whether he had cried last night for Sally, or would cry later when his grief came upon him, they didn't know. But the killing of Sluggo had clearly taken Karl by surprise and seemed to be one loss more than he could handle.

Tenderloin Tommy Dragovich and his enforcer Gundar were known by the cops who patrolled the Tenderloin. Fagetti thought Gundar was a viable suspect for the crime. This promising lead was worked for more than a week, trying to connect either of the men to the killings. When interviewed, Gundar said he'd been drinking in the 288 Club at the time of the crime. This lie was backed up by Tommy and the night bartender.

The forensics work didn't turn up any unexplained fingerprints on the knife or in the apartment. If Sally and Randy hadn't killed each other, then their killer had been experienced, careful or lucky. The case was going nowhere fast and new murders with more productive leads soon took precedence.

* * *

Sandy and Karl were both back to work at Compton's two days after the killings. For both of them, work was the only part of their lives that hadn't been irrevocably soiled by the murders.

Sandy, unfortunate enough to have seen the crime scene, shared what he knew with Karl. Either intentionally, or perhaps because his mind sought to protect them both, Sandy didn't describe or speculate about what the postures of the bodies suggested. He was sure their loved ones had died innocent of any sexual betrayal.

Sandy was the first to voice the thought, "We need to find out who did it, and then we'll make a plan."

"It was that dirty rotten Russian, Dragovich and his ape," Karl replied.

Sandy nodded in agreement; the street knew what the cops couldn't prove. The night following the killings, Gundar had been in Compton's between 2 and 3 a.m. when the trannies gathered. Gundar had made a point of mentioning the crime and hypothesizing about how 'bad things seem to happen to people that don't pay their rent.' He figured Tommy wanted a message sent. After all, his actions were worthless if nobody knew. He made sure the message got out, loud and clear.

"We say nothing to nobody," Sandy whispered, and reached across the small table offering his hand to Karl. They shook hands and sealed their bargain to find the killer and make a plan for revenge. Sandy knew this would be a long, hard process if they were going after Gundar and Tommy, the meanest and most powerful men in the Tenderloin.

* * *

August 29, 1966, two months after the double murder, was a hot night in the city. There was rioting in the black neighborhood of Hunter's Point, and Governor Reagan had called out the California National Guard. Tensions between the police and the community were high throughout the city.

In the Tenderloin, a few officers were known for abusing transgender people, and they were doing it tonight. Things began to boil over and Compton's was ground zero. Just like the blacks in Hunter's Point, the gays, trannies and subsistence sex workers had finally had enough. When the worst of the 'queen haters and baiters' as they were known, attempted to arrest a transgender woman at Compton's, she threw her coffee in the cop's face and the riot was on. Anything that could be thrown at the cops, from dishes to chairs, got tossed. Among the first casualties were the cafeteria's plate glass windows.

The riot inside Compton's expanded to the street and police reinforcements were called. The first patrol car to arrive was torched. Then the flames spread to a sidewalk newsstand two doors up Turk Street. Sandy and the waitresses were trying to stay out of the line of fire from the flying dishes and police clubs.

Karl chose to just keep working. A small alley separated the Compton's building from Karl and Sandy's apartment. The alley provided both access and storage for the garbage cans and the used cooking oil drum that was picked up and recycled. Tonight was Karl's regular night to change the oil in the deep fryer. The ten quarts of oil were still hot and he needed both hands to carry the large steel pot he used to collect the drained oil. Pushing the alley door open with his hip, he checked to make sure that the riot had not invaded the alley.

He peeked out from the alley to see who was winning— cops or queens. The riot filled the street on his left and the newsstand was ablaze just to his right. Beyond the halo of flames he saw Tommy and his ape Gundar standing in front of the 288 Club.

No one ever knew what—if anything—Karl thought about in the few seconds he took to walk over and throw the hot oil on the two figures. Their screams of surprise turned into screams of pain as the heat from the oil sank into their skin and clothing. The oil pot stayed where it fell when Karl went for his lighter and then tossed the open flame onto Tommy. In an instant Tommy was a human torch, and in his panic he ignited Gundar. Their eyes blinded by the oil and the pain, Tommy and Gundar whirled into each other and the front of the bar. Their flames quickly ignited the bar's striped awning.

It was not too long before some of the arriving police abandoned the riot and ran up Turk Street to the two flaming figures. Both men were curled up on the ground. As the flames dissipated, Karl thought the Russian and his ape were probably starting to look like Sluggo had when he'd curled up to die.

189

The first cop to arrive pulled Karl back from where he stood over the burned bodies. The cop, his face covered by a clear plastic shield, began to curse when he realized that Karl had been pissing on the bodies. Karl's stream had caught him on the ankle, darkening the deep blue of his riot gear.

"Do you want to help me put them out?" Karl asked the cop.

* * *

It took Sandy 90 minutes to drive from San Francisco to Vacaville where the state hospital for the criminally insane was located. Visiting day was Saturday, and he never missed seeing Karl. The big news during Karl's first year came when he stopped wearing his helmet.

"Karl, what, no helmet? You actually have hair. Who knew?"

"The doctors here are kind. They told me that they could remove the receiver from my head and the battery from in here." Karl tapped his abdomen to indicate the spot. "It's special psychic surgery that they do. They did it while I slept. No scars, no pain and now the Russians can't touch me."

"Karl, that's wonderful. And I have good news from the city, too. After the riot at Compton's, the Chronicle did a series on the police and the gay community. It didn't paint a pretty picture. This week the chief of police appointed their first ever Community Relations officer! His job is to be a bridge between the gay community and the police. They don't want another gay riot. We call him the fairy fuzz."

That was three years ago. But time really didn't seem to matter to Karl. If and when he was ever considered cured, he'd be going back to court to face the double murder charges.

"It's too bad that you can't play baseball here, like Randy and I did at Atascadero," said Sandy.

Karl sniffed and nodded.

"Yes, too bad, but they don't allow us to have bats." Then Karl leaned forward so that none of the other visitors or patients in the outside garden would hear.

"That's because some of the people here are crazy."

The End

Author's Notes

The 288 Club is set in San Francisco where I started as a fed. It uses true characters and events from the late 1960's and early 1970's. The Atascadero Gay encounter program, the riot at Compton's Cafeteria, the Tenderloin District, the 288 Club, the Cockettes and the appointment of the first community liaison officer to the gay community are all true. The Karl, Sally and Tenderloin Tommy characters are based on two supervisees of mine and a notorious crime boss. The Atascadero AGE program from 1962 was long ago discontinued, based on advances in our understanding of aberrant sexual behavior

Autobiography: Father and Son 1936

San Francisco

No good thing lasts forever. When Prohibition ended in 1933, Dad lost his successful bootlegging franchise at the Pacific Telephone Building.

He replaced his bootleg gin with the first nickel pinball machines in the city. The pinballs were more socially acceptable than his modest bookmaking operation, which had survived Prohibition. In San Francisco, besides a base level of crime – some violent, some not – there were also the more genteel illegalities that catered to the desires of the citizenry.

Not until my teens did I discover that the square boards hanging on the back of some pinball machines were for placing bets. The customer simply wrote his name and desired bet on the board.

Win or lose, both the customer and the bookmaker paid their debts faithfully. Illegal didn't mean uncivil. Welching on a bet was social suicide. Welch on a bet and you couldn't get a drink in a bar, hail a cab or borrow ten cents. In this city, at this time, it was illegal to make book, but it was a crime to welch on a bet.

When I was a kid, Sunday was our father-son day. I'd ride with Dad to visit the bars where he had pinball machines. He divided up the 24 bars so we made collection stops at six per week. His work clothes – wool slacks, a gabardine shirt and plaid Pendleton jacket – had absorbed the sweet smell of his Burley pipe tobacco.

Prince, our family dog, rode along every day with Dad. The big black and white cocker spaniel preferred to sit in the driver's lap, the better to hang his head out the window of the moving truck. At low speeds his floppy ears fluttered before being pinned back by the wind when we sped up.

Following Dad inside, I'd climb up on a bar stool for a Coke garnished with two maraschino cherries. Prince came in too and assumed a position at the foot of my stool. Dad placed Prince's beverage, a clean ash tray filled with beer, by the dog's side before taking up his own bourbon and water that customarily greeted his arrival. Once everyone was served the actual work began.

Dad emptied the coin box in each machine into a hand-cranked coin counter and then put the finished paper rolls in his jacket pocket. He consulted the square board that hung out of sight on the back of one pinball machine and noted something in a small book. Just before we left, the bartender always rewarded me with a small paper bag of candy. Lemon drops, candied ginger, Jordan almonds or gumballs. I passed him one of the thank-you notes Dad had put into envelopes before we left from home. The notes, unbeknownst to me at the time, were for the bookmaking and not Dad's pinball machines.

This ritual was interrupted only once. I was age nine, and we were collecting at the Kezar Club on Stanyan Street. The tavern's swinging doors opened and light cut through the dim interior. Officer Tom Sullivan, who was no stranger to us and the biggest man I had ever seen, filled the door. He came over to our place at the end of the bar. Dad always bought him a drink and, as always, passed him an envelope.

"Bill, it's always a pleasure to see you." Officer Sullivan smiled at Dad while he tousled my hair.

"Listen, I'm sorry, but the donation has to go up. It hasn't gone up in three years, so it's time."

"What are you thinking, Tom?"

"Ten bucks more a week should do and you're protected."

"Tom, times are hard. I'm not making what I used to before the Depression started. I'm sorry, but I can't donate more. Besides, if I raise you, then every other beat cop where I do any business will be expecting the same. I'm not saying that you'd go out and tell the other cops, but word would get around. You know that. I'm sorry" Dad turned to face the cop, his hands palm up, trying to explain and cajole.

"What can I say? I'm just a working stiff and if I don't get these little donations, I'm back to eating chuck steak and I really love eating tenderloin."

"Tom, I understand. I mean we're both just trying to make a living, but an extra ten bucks is unreasonable." With his hands flat on the bar, Dad grimaced and fixed Sullivan with his eyes.

"Bill, it's my beat. That's the new price of doing business. Take it or leave it!"

"Listen, you greedy Irish bastard, I'll go straight before I'll pay another dime!"

"Ah, Bill, you're embarrassing me, here. You and your boy will have to come with me now. You're under arrest for bookmaking." His index finger jabbed at the air in front of Dad's face.

Officer Sullivan let Dad lock his truck before he placed us in a police car he had summoned from the call-box on the corner.

"Take these two to the station. Bill here is a bookmaking collar. Hold the boy until his mother can pick him up."

Taking the candy bag from my hand, he poured the contents into his palm. A wad of money fell out from the bottom of the bag. Officer Sullivan dumped the candy back into the bag and handed it to me.

"Bill, I'm ashamed of you, corrupting your son. If you're not careful, he could grow up to be an attorney!"

I liked the police car ride and the police station better than Dad did. The officers sat me in a heavy oak chair opposite the desk sergeant and even gave me a Coke while I waited for Mom.

Dad's arrest made the news in the San Bruno Herald along with a neat booking photo. He had to pay a fine and lost some

194

of his bookmaking concessions. With a shrug and a smile, he told me it was "just the cost of doing business."

I got a mention in the paper, too. At the age of nine, I was famous. Some of my friends thought my adventure was exciting, even if their mothers didn't. Still, the best parts of the deal were my Sundays with Dad and the two cherries in my coke.

Author's Notes

Father and Son 1936 is a true story about my father. The bars, the candy bags and Dad's refusing to raise the protection bribe are all true.

About the Author

This collection of short stories is an outgrowth of Stu Scott's endeavor to deal with a PTSD issue through journaling as suggested by a VA counselor. After returning from the Air Force he worked as staff in a juvenile detention facility, moving on to adult probation and finally to federal probation and parole. Simultaneously, in 1980 he returned to the military as a reserve agent with the Army Criminal Investigation Command. Born and raised in the San Francisco bay area, he has lived with his wife in Moscow, Idaho since 1981. Believing that we only go around once in life and that one job is never enough, his other careers include: professional winemaker, college instructor, director of a school for disabled children and stained glass artist.

Questions or comments for Stu?

sls@turbonet.com

Also By This Author

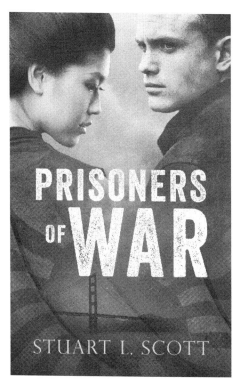

Pat McBride wants to marry his Japanese-American sweetheart
Bea Sakai. The public's growing hatred against all things Japanese
threatens the couple's plans. The Sakai flower shop is burned and
the family is interned. Pat's loyalties are now torn between duty to
his country and his love for Bea. What is he willing to do to win
her back?
Kirkus review says, "The author has a gift for sympathetic
portrayal of antagonistic views."
and
"An affecting, historically keen story."

Available at Amazon in paperback and on Kindle
ISBN: 9781732246829

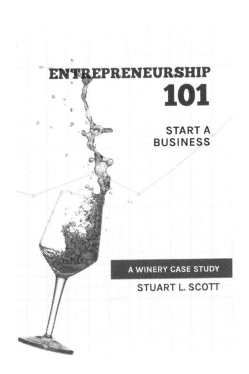

Why should you read this book? Do you want to start your own business, sell a product, or provide a valuable service? **Do you have a new business,** especially a small business? Do you like the idea of **learning from the insights and mistakes of others**? If you answered **YES** to any of these questions, then this book is for you. I learned long ago that I didn't have to be nearly as smart or creative, if I could steal the good ideas of others. This is your chance to do the same!

Available at Amazon in paperback and on Kindle

ISBN:9781732246843

68353385R00115

Made in the USA
Middletown, DE
21 September 2019